"The only thing I ask is that you let me talk to her first. Explain things in a way she'll understand."

"You mean make me look like the jerk who abandoned you and her?"

"I'll tell her the truth and make sure she understands that you didn't know about her. But she's nine, Luke. I have to pick the words carefully." She sighed. "Do you want to be there when I do? Keep me honest?"

She'd betrayed him in the most elemental way possible, so the word *honest* coming out of her beautiful mouth was hard to take. And the fact that he could still think she was beautiful felt wrong but couldn't be helped.

"After you tell her, I want time with her."

"Okay. I'll be in touch, Luke."

He wouldn't hold his breath on that but at least he knew where to find her.

Dear Reader,

It's said that no one gets out of this life without regrets. Hindsight is 20/20. "If I'd known then what I know now." There are probably more common expressions but those are the ones that popped into my mind. The point is that we all make decisions with consequences, but usually a consequence that looks exactly like us doesn't show up unexpectedly at the front door. This is what happens to Luke McCoy in *Daughter on His Doorstep*.

Ten years ago he was a screwup in love with Shelby Richards, the girl next door. He felt she deserved a better man than him and broke up with her, then enlisted in the army. But he had to see her one last time to say goodbye.

At that meeting, Shelby planned to tell him she was pregnant with his child. Before she could, Luke said he was leaving for basic training, and she didn't want to get in the way of the new life he was making. Ten years later he's back and his daughter knocks on the door, demanding to know if he's really her father.

It was exhilarating to write Luke and Shelby's story. I hope you enjoy their bumpy ride from mutual distrust to acceptance and finally the realization that they never stopped loving each other.

Happy reading!

Teresa Southwick

Daughter
on His Doorstep

Teresa Southwick

HARLEQUIN
SPECIAL
EDITION

HARLEQUIN®
SPECIAL EDITION™

Recycling programs
for this product may
not exist in your area.

ISBN-13: 978-1-335-89438-0

Daughter on His Doorstep

Copyright © 2020 by Teresa Southwick

Harlequin Enterprises ULC
22 Adelaide St. West, 40th Floor
Toronto, Ontario M5H 4E3, Canada
www.Harlequin.com

Printed in U.S.A.

Teresa Southwick lives with her husband in Las Vegas, the city that reinvents itself every day. An avid fan of romance novels, she is delighted to be living out her dream of writing for Harlequin.

I want to acknowledge two amazing women who answered some important questions for this book.

Much gratitude to army specialist Tiffany Rubecamp for information about basic training.
And thank you for your service.

Much appreciation to Taylor Boyle for your input on children's computer tablets.
Lucy and Parker are so lucky you're their mom!

Chapter One

Luke McCoy was back.

Like a bad rash. Or a bad dream. Everything bad.

From her upstairs bedroom window Shelby Richards had a view of the house next door where he grew up. She happened to glance out and saw a man carrying a bulky duffel bag up the walkway. Something about his loose-limbed, sexy stride was familiar and a shiver of awareness made her look closer. He was broader and more muscular than he'd been ten years ago. But that was definitely Luke.

Don't panic, she told herself, but it was hard not to.

The man didn't have any idea she'd had his baby.

All those feelings from a decade ago came back

to her now. She'd been seventeen, pregnant, scared and ashamed because she was going to have a baby before high school graduation. She'd wanted to tell him but when you're a pregnant teenager who broke the rules, you don't have a lot of choices except to do what you're told.

"Shelby, what's wrong?" Her mother stood in the doorway. Pam Richards had a laundry basket resting against her hip. "You look as if you've seen a ghost."

"Luke. Luke McCoy, the guy I used to—"

"I remember who he is." The temperature of her mother's voice could freeze water.

"He's next door. Right now." Did that thready, whispery voice belong to her? "It looks like he's moving in. After he left, his mother rented the house. When she moved out a few weeks ago I thought that was it. Why would he be back now?"

"I don't know." Pam set the basket down just inside the doorway.

There was an unyielding hardness in her mother's brown eyes that Shelby recognized all too well. She'd felt the power of it many times but never more than when she'd confessed her pregnancy and admitted Luke McCoy, the one guy she'd been forbidden to see, was the father. What her mother said next was like a slap. *If you'd stayed away from that loser like I told you, you wouldn't be in this mess.*

The only person who'd escaped "the look" was Emma. Her beautiful little girl, her pride and joy. She was precocious and independent was her middle name. And her grandmother adored her. Now she was…

"Where's Emma?" Shelby lowered her voice and glanced toward the empty doorway.

"She's downstairs in the family room watching a movie." Pam spoke softly and moved closer. They both looked out the window and watched him carry clothes on hangers into the house.

"Yup. Definitely moving in." Shelby's heart was hammering as apprehension trickled through her. "He's going to be right next door. How can he not see her? And what will happen when he does? You know she looks just like him," Shelby said.

"Only because you know he's her father."

"You should have let me tell him, Mom."

"He was wild and reckless and headed to hell in a handbasket. You were an honor student with no-where to go but up. Now you're a respected high school math teacher but you wouldn't be if you'd told him. He would have ruined your life. And Emma's."

Shelby glared at the man walking back to his truck where the bed was full of boxes. His dark hair was short and his arms tan. The dark T-shirt was snug across his shoulders and worn jeans hugged his lean hips and strong legs. Her memory filled in the dark brown eyes and lean, handsome features. She'd been an innocent rule follower who never de-fied her mother but resisting Luke McCoy had been impossible. She was a moth to his flame. A bee to his honey—exciting because he was everything she wasn't. A rule breaker, a rebel. Fearless. Independent.

"But he's her father, Mom. And he's moving in next door."

"Shelby, honey, I've always taken care of you. After your father left and started a new family it was just the two of us. And I'm so proud of you."

"Except when I was pregnant. There was a time you wouldn't even look at me."

"I'll admit it was a shock when you told me you were going to have a baby. But we got through it together. And I couldn't be more proud of you. You finished high school at the top of your class and went to college. Graduated summa cum laude. And you did it while raising Emma."

"I couldn't have done it without you, Mom."

But she would never forget the resentment she'd felt. Being forced to keep a secret. Then Emma was born and Pam was there. Always. Her biggest cheerleader. Her support system. Babysitter. Loving grandmother. Shelby had been busy and never let herself think about Luke because it hurt too much.

"I never told you this, but I saw him. Before he left."

"What? When?" Pam's voice was sharp. "You said he broke up with you."

"He did. But he contacted me, wanted to talk. I sneaked out to meet him." She met her mother's shocked gaze and braced herself, then looked back at Luke. "I was going to tell him the truth. He had a right to know."

"But you didn't." It was both statement and question.

"Before I could, he told me he enlisted in the army. He was leaving."

"You did the right thing, Shelby."

She couldn't look away as he made trips back and forth from the truck to the house, unloading all those boxes. Never once did he glance over.

Couldn't he feel her staring? He'd once told her she was all he had. After his dad died in the car accident, his mother blamed him for reasons Shelby didn't understand. His relationship with his mom was fractured and Shelby promised he'd always have her. And he vowed to always have her back but he broke that promise.

"I'm not so sure I did do the right thing. Emma has been asking about her father." And Shelby had been giving her vague answers. Stuff like him joining the army, or he couldn't be with her weren't cutting it. She was nine years old and starting to want details, facts. Now he was here. It was complications on steroids. "I can't imagine a scenario where he doesn't see her and figure out that she's his daughter."

"His mother didn't suspect," Pam pointed out.

"After Luke and I broke up she ignored me. It was like this house didn't exist. Then he left for the army and renters moved in. She was only there in between to get it ready for the next ones. I don't think she ever saw Emma. If she did, it's possible she just didn't want to know about her."

"Maybe. But don't borrow trouble. There's no reason to believe he won't ignore us, too."

"Seriously, Mom?" Shelby glanced at Pam and in her peripheral vision she thought a shadow moved on the wall in the hallway. "Emma?"

Quickly she went to the doorway and looked out but there was no sign of the little girl. She walked back to the window. "When you bury your head in the sand you leave your ass exposed. I need to tell Luke, get ahead of this. Tell the truth and get out from under this secret I've carried for so long."

Just then she saw her strong-willed little secret march across the driveway and head to the house next door. She knocked and Luke answered.

"Oh, God…" Shelby knew it was time to panic now.

Luke McCoy looked down at the little girl standing on the porch. She had dark hair and eyes that were spitting with attitude. As if someone had recently ticked her off. She was probably selling something for a school fundraiser and getting turned down. But the cop in him took issue with the fact that her parents were letting her go door-to-door all by herself.

"Hi," he said. "Can I help you?"

"Are you my father?"

That was not what he expected. "Am I what now?"

"My father. I heard mommy and Grammy say the man next door is my father. So, are you?"

Luke was a detective with the Huntington Hills Police Department. He was usually the one doing the interrogating. To say her question took him by surprise was an understatement and he was momentarily at a loss for words.

"I'm waiting." There was annoyance in her dark eyes and stubbornness written all over her face.

A face that seemed familiar somehow. "Who's your mother? Where do you live? What's your name? How old are you?"

"Emma Richards. I live next door." She pointed. "My mom is Shelby Richards. And I'm nine."

Luke felt as if this little bit of a kid had just gut punched him. A quick mental calculation made the timing work and he studied her more closely. The obstinate line of her jaw. An angry tilt of her head. That glint in her eyes warning of the rebellion raging inside. He was shocked, angry and a whole bunch of other feelings, but, oddly enough, surprise wasn't one of them. The kid looked like him. She had the same indentation in her chin, her eyes and the shape of her brows were the image of his.

"Emma…"

Shelby raced up the walkway and pulled the little girl protectively against her side. For the second time in as many minutes Luke had that two-by-four to the gut feeling. Talk about a blast from the past. He saw

Shelby's mother standing back, but the dragon lady was watching and itching to interfere. The woman had hated him ten years ago and judging by the look on her face nothing had changed.

"What are you doing here?" Shelby asked the kid.

Emma looked up. "I heard you and Grammy talking about him."

"That's eavesdropping." Shelby's tone was matter-of-fact rather than disapproving. "We've talked about this."

"I know. I'm sorry. But I couldn't help it and you can give me a time-out from TV." She moved away and there was a pleading look in her eyes. "Just tell me. Is he my father?"

"I'd like to know the answer to that, too." Luke met her gaze.

To her credit Shelby answered in that same even tone. "Yes."

Luke and Emma stared at each other. It felt all kinds of wrong for a father and daughter to find out about each other at the same time. When she was nine. She looked as defensive as he felt. And there was a very long, very awkward silence before Shelby broke it.

She went down on one knee and took the little girl's hands into her own. "Look, peanut, I need you to go home with Grammy while I talk to Luke."

"That's his name?" She glanced up at him.

He nodded. "I'm Luke McCoy."

"I don't want to go home." Emma's small face was full of determination and defiance.

"I understand that. And this is a lot to take in. But I'm asking you for a few minutes. Then you and I will talk."

"Promise?"

"Cross my heart." Shelby made the sign over the left side of her chest. "Now go home with Grammy, please."

"Okay." Emma's expression was full of confusion and resentment but she left without another word.

Luke didn't know what to say. Shouldn't a father know how to talk to his child? Shouldn't it be instinctive? And the feelings. The love. Wasn't that automatic? But not so much. The kid was a complete stranger to him. And that was Shelby's fault.

Luke felt the anger rise. "How dare you—"

She gave him a look then held up a finger to shut him up as Emma held her grandmother's hand and headed for the house next door. The little girl glanced over her shoulder at him before disappearing inside.

"Okay," Shelby said. "Now you can say whatever you have to."

She met his gaze directly but uneasiness swirled in her light brown eyes with green and gold flecks. He'd forgotten how one or the other color dominated when she was happy, angry or sad. She'd been a girl the last time he saw her but was all woman now, slender and curvy at the same time. Her straight brown hair was streaked with highlights and fell past her shoulders. She was more beautiful than he remembered. In the past he'd loved the dimples in her cheeks when she smiled at him, but she wasn't smiling now.

"I don't need your permission to speak," he said.

"Under these circumstances you do. When my daughter is present—"

"Our daughter," he snapped. "How could you have kept this from me? I had a right to know."

"I was young and scared."

At least she didn't tell him he was wrong. "But why didn't you tell me?"

"So many reasons." She wasn't the least bit defensive, which was surprising. She was taking responsibility for what she'd done. "You broke up with me and my mom had forbidden me to see you—"

"That's no excuse."

"Let me finish." She looked down at her feet, then met his gaze. "That last time I saw you, when you wanted to meet, I actually planned to defy my mother and tell you I was pregnant."

"She didn't want you to tell me the truth?"

"More than that. She gave me an ultimatum—if I said anything, I'd have to find somewhere else to live."

"She would never have thrown you out." He wasn't sure how he knew or why he was actually defending the woman who never hid her dislike of him.

"I was in no position to risk calling her bluff. Not

with a baby to think about. But, believe it or not, I planned to go against her and tell you."

"But you didn't."

"No. Before I could you said you'd enlisted in the army because you were lost, struggling. You and your mother didn't get along and your life had no purpose. So you signed a recruitment contract."

"If I'd known about the baby, I might have been able to change things."

"My body, my life," she said. "I was pregnant and my body was going to change. I accepted those consequences. But you were making plans for your life and I didn't want to be the reason those plans didn't work out."

"So you're a saint and I'm a sinner?" Luke saw her flinch at his jab but it wasn't as satisfying as he'd expected.

"I probably deserve that but lashing out at me isn't going to change anything." Then her mouth pulled tight and regret hovered in her eyes for a moment. "Whether you like it or not, we share a daughter. What are you going to do about it?"

"I have an obligation to her."

"She's a blessing in every way, not a duty." There was steel in her voice. Mother lion in full-on protection mode.

"That's not what I meant and you know it."

"Do I?" One delicate eyebrow lifted. "I haven't seen you in years. How would I know what your priorities are? I haven't seen much of your mother either."

"Because she rented out the house. Now she wants to sell and I'm here to fix it up and handle the details for her. She moved to an adult community in Phoenix."

"So your relationship hasn't improved in all this time. You couldn't be under the same roof during that process?"

Although they never talked about the past, he and his mom were actually getting along better. Maybe because he wasn't an angry, aimless jerk. "She was in a hurry to move on with the next part of her life and I offered to help."

Shelby nodded. "That's your issue and none of my business, really. But Emma is my priority. And judging by your self-righteous indignation, you want to be in her life."

"Of course." The answer was automatic.

"Do you want me to smooth the process of getting to know her? Be a go-between to make it easier?"

"No." That was automatic *and* adamant. He didn't want anything from her. "I can handle it."

"Okay then. The only thing I ask is that you let me talk to her first. Explain things in a way she'll understand."

"You mean make me look like the jerk who abandoned you and her?"

"I'll tell her the truth and make sure she understands that you didn't know about her. But she's nine,

Luke. I have to pick the words carefully." She sighed. "Do you want to be there when I do? Keep me honest?"

She'd betrayed him in the most elemental way possible so the word *honest* coming out of her beautiful mouth was hard to take. And the fact that he could still think she was beautiful felt wrong, but couldn't be helped. Did he want to be there when she talked to Emma?

"I— You better." He had no idea what to say because he didn't know anything about her. That was on Shelby. "After you tell her, I want time with her."

"Okay." They exchanged phone numbers and she promised to call and set up a meeting between them right away. "I'll be in touch, Luke."

He wouldn't hold his breath on that but at least he knew where to find her. And that was all he knew about this Shelby Richards. She'd been a gifted student years ago but he had no clue what she did for a living. Speaking of living, she was still at her mom's which led him to believe she wasn't married. That didn't mean there wasn't a man in her life. His primitive negative reaction to that was a complete surprise. His long-ago rebellion rose up and resisted that thought.

But this day had been weird. He found out he was a father and his kid was nine years old. It made an odd kind of sense that his reaction to his long-ago love was weird, too. No way could he care for a woman who had lied to him in the most basic way by not telling him she was going to have his child.

Nope. Their only connection in the future would be handing off that child because now that he finally knew about Emma, he had nine years to make up for.

As she walked next door, Shelby could feel Luke's stare burning a hole in her back. Seeing him again was surreal. The passion in him that mesmerized her before was still there. Unfortunately it was fueled by his hostility toward her now, because of what she'd done. One could hardly blame him. She wanted badly to believe she'd done what was right but just a little while ago she'd questioned her actions while she and her mother peeked out the window at him.

Oh what a tangled web we weave when first we practice to deceive.

The first step in untangling this mess was to tell Emma the truth and put it into some context that a nine-year-old could wrap her head around. This might be the first time ever that she'd wished to be gifted with words instead of math. How was she going to explain all this to a child who didn't know about the birds and bees yet? She was hoping to postpone that conversation for as long as possible to preserve her innocence. Emma was a little girl, too young to understand wanting someone more than your next breath. So painfully in love that you had to give yourself to him and damn the consequences.

"Stick to the facts," Shelby mumbled to herself. She opened the front door and walked inside.

Her mother was waiting for her. "Well?"

"What?"

"Luke. What did he say?"

That man bubbled and churned like a volcano about to erupt and it had been irresistible to a seventeen-year-old girl. A few minutes ago she'd seen emotions stirring, making his eyes dark as coals, but he'd kept himself in check. Clearly he was shocked, angry and sarcastic but his responses and questions were completely reasonable. All things considered.

"The guy I remember wouldn't have been so restrained."

"I don't know what that means." Her mother's eyes narrowed suspiciously.

"He wants to get to know Emma. And he has every right." Shelby added that because she expected pushback.

"But is that good for her?" Pam folded her arms over her chest. "We don't know anything about him."

"Mom—"

"Don't 'Mom' me. He was willful and wild. He had more than one brush with the law. Do you want your child with a man like that? Does he have a job? Will he be a bad influence on her? She's just a baby."

"I wish she was. This would be so much easier."

Shelby loved her mother and was grateful for everything she'd done. But there were times she wanted her to be wrong. This time she wasn't. "Let's put aside the question of what's good for her until it becomes relevant. She's been asking questions about her father and now she knows the truth. Plus there's Luke to consider. He's her father and keeping her from him is not just wrong. It could create problems."

"Such as?"

"He could sue for legal rights. What if he tries to take her away from me because I kept her from him?"

Pam's face went white. "He wouldn't."

"I'm not willing to push the issue and find out." Shelby's head was starting to pound. "Let's take this one step at a time. The first thing I have to do is explain this situation to Emma as best I can."

"Maybe you should talk to the school counselor first."

At the high school where Shelby taught math there was a counselor who helped kids academically, socially and emotionally. She was a good friend and it was an excellent suggestion. Unfortunately Shelby didn't think Emma would tolerate a delay while her mom discussed this with a mental health care professional. She would have to wing it.

"This has waited long enough and I don't think she'll be put off. She's willful and stubborn like Luke. She's also angry and confused." The expression on her girl's face was just like his. Now that she thought about it, he must have seen the resemblance because he never asked if Emma was his child. "I'll tell her now."

"Just answer her questions," Pam said. "She's going to have a lot."

That was good advice. Her mother knew Emma almost as well as she did. "You're right. I'll give her the broad strokes and let her ask whatever she wants. She can only grasp so much right now. As she gets older things will occur to her and she'll probably want to know more until Luke being around is the new normal."

"If he sticks around." Pam shrugged. "He left once. There's no reason to believe he won't do it again."

Shelby couldn't deny that and now that Emma knew about him she would be affected if he left. She made a mental note to find out what his intentions were.

"Where is Emma?"

"She went straight to her room," her mother answered.

Shelby took a deep breath. "Wish me luck."

Slowly she walked upstairs, testing out what to say, how to open this explosive dialogue. Everything she came up with was so lame it made her want to slap herself. In the second room on the left, Emma was sitting on the carpet by her bed. She was holding the ragged stuffed bear she always grabbed when she was upset. The sheer number of stuffed animals in her room was impressive but she had two go-tos. A koala Grammy bought her on a trip to San Diego that she slept with. And this one with a missing eye and a rip in his foot was for emotional support. It looked sad and anxious, just like Emma did now.

Shelby glanced around the room with its pale pink walls and white-painted doors and baseboards. Lace curtains crisscrossed the window. A white wooden chest that held dolls and their clothes along with games sat underneath. The twin bed was neatly made with a princess-themed spread and matching throw pillows.

She loved this child more than anything and had mostly forgotten the time when she was pregnant and afraid because when Emma was born it was love at first sight. It seemed impossible for that feeling to get bigger, yet it had. And just like that she knew how to open this conversation that needed to happen.

"I love you, baby girl." She sat down on the rug in front of her child. "Before you were born I loved you, but when they put you in my arms—when I saw that sweet round face and those tiny hands and feet, the love was so big—"

"Bigger than the ocean?" Emma loved hearing about the day she was born.

"Way bigger. To the moon and back," she answered.

"Was he there when I was born?" The little girl glanced toward the window that looked out on the house next door where her father was moving in.

"Like he told you… His name is Luke McCoy. And no, he wasn't there."

"Why? Where was he?"

"He joined the army and went away." Shelby remembered her mother's advice about answering questions and stopped there.

Emma clutched the bear tighter to her chest. "Did he have to be a soldier?"

She thought about how to respond to that because answers had nuance. "No. He went voluntarily."

"How come?" Dark eyes—Luke's eyes—stared at her, trying to understand.

"Well—" She wanted to be honest without negativity impacting a little girl's opinion and future relationship with the father she'd just met. Words mattered and she chose them carefully. "He didn't know what he wanted to do with his life. So he decided to be a soldier and serve his country while he figured that out."

Shelby glanced at the doorway where her own mother now stood. The two of them had raised this girl together and she loved her, too. But she sent her a look, a warning to not say anything. Pam moved her head slightly, showing she understood.

Emma didn't respond for a few moments, then finally asked, "Is he still a soldier?"

"I don't know." There was so much to take in she hadn't thought about it. She had no idea what he did for a living, or anything else about him since the last time she'd seen him.

"Why don't you know?"

Shelby knew her child, knew there were multiple questions layered into that single one. Her group of friends all had fathers who'd been around their whole lives. Emma was different and in her nine-year-old experience Shelby knew everything. So there had to be a reason she didn't know this.

"Peanut, when I was expecting you, your father and I weren't married."

"How come?"

A billion reasons, but she wouldn't understand any of them. Shelby came up with what she thought would be the easiest thing for Emma to take in. "I still had to finish high school and Luke, your father, had to go in the army because he signed a contract promising he would."

She looked puzzled and her mouth trembled a little, an indication her feelings were hurt. "My friend Natalie's father went away for work and he called her every day. She could see him on the computer. And he could see her. Maybe soldiers don't have computers."

Shelby couldn't and wouldn't let this be on Luke. It was all her and her mom. She glanced at Pam and saw the negative head movement. Nope, this time she wasn't going to throw him under the bus.

She took a deep breath. "Baby, your father didn't know about you. That's why he didn't call."

Dark eyes grew wide. "You didn't tell him I was in your tummy?"

"No." Please don't ask how you got in there, Shelby prayed.

"Why not?"

"I know you hate it when grown-ups say it's complicated but it is. And you're too young to understand all the reasons. So this is one of those times I have to say it. He had to go away. There was no way for him to get out of it. And I thought it would be easier for him if he didn't have to worry about things at home."

"You mean the way Karen worries about Buster when they go see her grandma and grandpa?"

Shelby smiled. "Buster is a dog so that's a little different, but it was kind of like that." Shelby watched emotions tumble and roll through the big, dark eyes and hoped this would be sufficient for now.

Finally Emma nodded and her expression brightened a little. "He lives next door now?"

"He's going to fix up the house for his mother."

"The lady who used to live there?"

"I'm not sure which one you mean because the house has been rented several times to different families. But your father's mother owns it." The woman who was her other grandmother. Shelby just realized this nightmare was like quicksand. For every step forward she sank a little deeper and felt a whole lot worse. "After he fixes it up he's going to sell it for her."

"That means he'll move away, too?"

"Yes." Shelby was pretty sure this conversation had moved beyond the past and was heading into "what do we do now" territory. "He wants to get to know you, Emma."

"Really?" She suddenly sounded hesitant and looked uncertain.

"He made that very clear." Along with the fact that he was mad as hell at Shelby.

"But you don't have to do anything you don't want to." Pam spoke for the first time.

Emma toyed with her bear's only remaining button eye. "I guess I want to see him, Grammy."

"Are you sure, sweetie? You do have a choice."

Shelby knew that tone in her mother's voice. The one where the words were right but there was an implied warning, a hint that said don't do it.

Shelby looked at her daughter and put all the reassurance possible into her smile. "You think it over, kiddo. If you want to see him I will make it happen."

"Okay." She stood. "Can I watch cartoons while I think?"

"Yes."

Shelby stood, too, and watched her little girl walk slowly out of the room. Moments later faint noise from downstairs indicated she'd turned on the TV. This time she would make sure Emma didn't overhear the rest of this conversation.

She moved close to her mom who was still in the doorway and kept an eye on the hallway. "Mom, he's her father. He wants to see her and I won't stand in the way."

"Shelby, he's trouble—"

"He's an adjustment for her and for me. Not trouble. Not yet. I'm not sure what legal rights he has, if any, but I'm going to find out. At this point there's nothing to be gained by backing him into a corner. The Luke I remember wouldn't take it well."

"We'll get an attorney—"

"If she decides she wants to see him, Mom, I'm going to let her. I never want her to wonder about him. After that we'll just deal with whatever happens."

"I hope you know what you're doing."

"So do I."

Chapter Two

Dinner at the Richardses' house that night was about as much fun as a wardrobe malfunction in an algebra class of teenagers looking for any distraction from math. Shelby was caught between her mother's obvious disapproval and Emma's curiosity and confusion at the prospect of having a father. It was hard being the one in the middle who could see both sides.

"What is he like? My dad?" Emma picked up a chicken leg from her plate and took a bite.

"I honestly don't know now." Shelby pushed her own food around. With her stomach in knots she didn't have much appetite. "It's been ten years since I last saw him. People change."

"Not that much. Leopards don't change their

spots." Her mother's mouth twisted as if the broccoli she'd just eaten was a sour lemon.

·"You don't like him, Grammy?"

"I didn't say that." Pam got Shelby's warning look and backed off. "It's just that he had some growing up to do."

"I wonder if he likes soccer," Emma mused.

It was her current sports obsession. She was athletic, a trait from Luke. He played high school football and baseball while Shelby tripped over her own feet. "If he doesn't know the game you can teach him about it. I'm sure he'd like to learn about anything you're interested in."

Emma suddenly looked uncertain. "How do you know? Does he have other kids?"

"That's a very good question," her mother said with a little too much enthusiasm. "It's possible. And he might have a wife, too."

Neither of those possibilities had occurred to Shelby, which was stupid. Just because she hadn't found anyone who wanted to be an instant father didn't mean he hadn't fallen in love, married and started a family. She'd been watching the house all day and hadn't seen anyone else go in, but that didn't mean he was single.

Or he could be a serial killer. It wasn't that crazy. What did she know about him now? One thing she knew for sure, though. Before her child spent time with Luke McCoy, Shelby wanted an interview with him. That was going to happen tonight after

Emma went to bed and her mom was upstairs reading. Luke had turned her comfortable world upside down but family routine brought a little bit of order to her chaos.

"Mommy, I'm full." Emma's plate was empty of chicken and tater tots. All that remained was her untouched broccoli.

"You didn't eat your vegetables."

"I forgot to save room. Sorry, Mom." She didn't look the least bit sorry.

This was a familiar scenario. Shelby would threaten to ground her and take away privileges. Usually Emma negotiated eating one or two "trees" and everyone was happy. Shelby didn't have the energy tonight. She skipped all the steps and went straight for the nuclear option.

"Are you willing to give up ice cream for dessert?" It was Emma's all-time favorite.

The little girl thought for a moment, then nodded. "Grammy got chocolate and I don't like it that much. Vanilla is better."

"Okay, then. You may be excused." Shelby added, "It's time for your bath."

"But we just had dinner." The drama in her tone was not unexpected.

"We ate late tonight." That was a normal consequence when the guy who fathered your child unexpectedly moved back into the house next door. "And the longer you talk back, the less TV time you have. The clock is ticking, peanut. Don't forget to clear your plate."

The little girl carried it to the sink, then hurried out of the room and stomped up the stairs to the bathroom.

Shelby looked across the table at her mother's barely touched plate. "Are you feeling all right?"

"I could ask you the same thing."

"Yeah, I didn't feel much like eating either," she admitted.

"You're going to talk to him, aren't you?" her mother asked. "Don't look so surprised. I know you pretty well, after all. And your face went white when I said he might be married." Pam pushed her plate away and rested her arms on the table. She suddenly looked older and it had nothing to do with the silver strands of hair running through her brunette bob.

The woman was right and it was a waste of energy to deny it. "I was going to wait until Emma was in bed and you were settled upstairs. But yes, I plan to find out more about him before letting him into Emma's life."

"He's back for less than twenty-four hours and you're already sneaking out to see him again." Pam frowned. "Do you see why I'm concerned?"

"I just didn't want you to worry." Mostly.

The woman almost smiled. "Shelby, you're a mother. Tell me you wouldn't worry about Emma under the same circumstances."

She shook her head. "Of course you're right."

"This is an impossible situation and you're doing what you think you have to. All I ask is that you don't sneak around behind my back."

Like you did with him before. She didn't say the words but Shelby heard them all the same. "I won't, Mom." She stood and started gathering plates to clear the table. "I'll do the dishes before going over there—"

"No. Let me. You should just go and get it over with." Pam took the plates and walked to the sink. "I'll make sure Emma doesn't stay in the tub too long."

"Okay. Thanks, Mom."

The woman glanced over her shoulder and gave her "the look."

"Don't make me regret this."

Shelby didn't know what to say to that so she said nothing before heading to the front door. It was January and even in Southern California it was chilly this time of year. Halfway to Luke's house she was sorry she hadn't grabbed a jacket. Or maybe the prospect of confronting Luke was making her colder than the weather.

How ironic. Ten years ago her whole world had revolved around being alone with Luke McCoy and every time except the last time, seeing him had made her hot all over. But that was then, this was now and it wasn't about him. It was about her daughter. Correction: their daughter. She'd better get used to that.

At his front door she knocked. Her long-sleeved

T-shirt and jeans weren't much protection against the cold wind blowing from the north. She glanced over her shoulder and made sure his truck was at the curb, proof that he was inside. She was about to ring the bell when the porch light went on and temporarily blinded her as the door opened.

"Shelby." Luke's voice was deep and disapproving.

Still, her body involuntarily responded, some sort of muscle memory or something, because tingles danced over her skin and settled in her chest.

"I need to talk to you, Luke."

"About?"

"Emma, of course." There was nothing else that connected them.

"So you changed your mind. You're not going to let me see her." It wasn't a question and sounded as if he'd been expecting this.

"No. At least not unless—" She didn't quite know how to phrase the question.

He waited for her to finish the thought and when she didn't he asked, "Unless what?"

Standing on the porch she started to shiver. "I don't know you anymore, Luke. What if you're a fugitive from justice? Or a serial killer."

One corner of his mouth lifted for a moment. That seemed to amuse him.

"Something funny?" she asked.

"No. Please continue."

"I can't let you spend time with her until I'm sure it's okay. She's my child—"

"Mine, too."

She'd been right about him staking out his biological claim. "Yours, too. But I don't know what you've been doing since you left town, joined the army—" She suddenly started to shake from the cold and couldn't get out the words.

"Damn it. I guess you better come inside."

She nodded and stepped over the threshold, grateful to be out of the cold. But the relief didn't last nearly long enough. He closed the door then walked through the living room furnished with only a battered brown recliner chair and several empty boxes. She followed him to the kitchen and saw an open beer on the island next to a boxed frozen dinner.

He saw where she was looking. "Do you want a beer?"

"No, thanks. I don't like it." On top of being pregnant last time they saw each other, she hadn't been old enough to drink. He had no way of knowing what she liked.

His dark eyes smoldered as he considered her, most likely with resentment. "I bet you're a wine woman."

"Yes." That was kind of a surprise. But it reminded her that this was a two-way street. "I realize that you know nothing about me either. So let me start. I finished high school while I was pregnant with Emma, then went to college. While raising her I took classes and got my degree in mathematics with an emphasis on teaching. Now I teach Advanced Placement algebra and calculus at Huntington Hills High."

"I know."

"What?" She stood on the other side of the island from him. "How could you possibly know that?"

He folded his arms over a broad chest and the sleeves of his bad boy black T-shirt tightened around his muscular biceps. "I ran a background check on you."

"Excuse me? How could you do that?"

"Because I found out I have a daughter and you didn't see fit to tell me." His eyes flashed with anger.

"No. I mean that literally. How are you able to run a background check on someone unless you're a—"

"Cop." His mouth pulled tight for a moment. "Yeah, not a serial killer."

"I didn't really think that. It's just that when it comes to you all I have are question marks. Are you married? Do you have a family? Children?"

"No. No. And yes. One child. Her name is Emma and I just found out today." He took a sip of beer, then set it down on the white-tiled island. "I'm guessing you're not married."

"How do you know?"

"Other than the fact that you still live with your mother? It was in the background check." He shrugged. "Being a detective has its perks."

"Okay then. Obviously my mother is not your favorite person, but she helped me through a difficult time." She saw his eyes harden. "If not for her I couldn't have gone to school after you left and never looked back."

"I wrote to you." His voice was soft but every word was like a sledgehammer.

"What?"

"In basic training we got one phone call home to let family know we arrived. Then our only means of communicating was through letters. I wrote to you."

She didn't think he was making it up, but she said, "I never got any letters."

"That doesn't mean I didn't write them."

He watched her while she processed that information. If he was telling the truth, there was only one explanation for her not getting them. One going astray she could understand, but all of them? Her mother must have intercepted them. But she wouldn't do that. And Shelby couldn't go there.

"How was the army?" she asked instead.

For a moment it looked as if he would push back, but he didn't. "I was an MP—military police. A lot of people who knew me way back when thought it was a cosmic joke."

"You followed in your father's footsteps." She remembered his dad was a police detective.

That got a look of surprise and for a moment chased away his veneer of antagonism. For those few seconds he was the Luke she'd once found irresistible. And that was unsettling.

"Yeah, I did." And then the frown was back. "But you'll probably want proof."

He walked over to the kitchen table and picked up his wallet and something else, then handed them to her. "My Huntington Hills PD identification and detective shield."

"It looks a lot like a driver's license, but the badge appears to be pretty official." She handed them back.

"Actually, you can buy a badge on the internet."

"Did you?"

"No. I got it the old-fashioned way, by graduating from the police academy, then putting in my time on patrol before passing the detective's exam. I can give you references."

"That won't be necessary." Luke was a lot of things, but not a liar. She could see that he was the real deal.

"So I pass inspection."

"With flying colors," she said.

"Then I guess we're done here." He seemed to be in a hurry to get rid of her.

"Not quite. Emma wants to spend time with you. I'd like to set up a meeting as soon as possible."

"How about tomorrow? It's Sunday. I'm off."

Wow, that was soon. But Shelby knew she didn't really have a choice. "Okay. I'll bring her over. How about noon?"

"Fine."

No, it wasn't fine. Not even in the same zip code as fine. But Shelby didn't see a way out.

* * *

The next day there was a knock on the door just as the digital clock on the stove said 12:00. "She was always punctual," Luke muttered to himself.

He had to be a dad now with no clue how to do that. When Emma had asked if he was her father and he realized it was true, a primal need to know her raged inside him. Now he had no earthly idea what to say to her. Talk about being thrown into the deep end of the pool.

Then the doorbell rang, startling him out of his inertia, and he walked through the house and answered the door. Shelby stood there with Emma's hand clutched in her own. He was furious with the mother but tamped it down and smiled at his daughter.

"Hi."

"Hi." She looked more than a little uncertain.

"Let's do a proper introduction," Shelby said. "Emma, this is your father, Luke McCoy. Luke this is your daughter, Emma Rose."

"It's nice to meet you, Emma. This is kind of weird, huh?"

She nodded but didn't say anything.

"Do you want to come in?" he asked her.

"Sure."

His daughter pulled her hand from her mother's and walked inside. Shelby started to follow but he moved in front of her and she collided with his chest. For a split second he automatically wanted to wrap his arms around her and it stirred up memories from a lifetime ago. He hated himself for remembering.

"This is my time," he said so only Shelby could hear.

"I know. It's just—" She sighed and peeked around him. "Hey, peanut, do you want me to stay with you?"

"That's okay, Mommy. You can go."

"You're sure?"

"She's sure," Luke said. "Right?"

"Yes," Emma answered.

Shelby stared at him for a moment with her bottom lip caught between her teeth. She looked so much like the seventeen-year-old sad and lost girl he'd said goodbye to. It had killed him to leave her and hadn't taken long to realize he'd made a mistake cutting her loose. Now he knew she was a liar and he'd dodged a bullet. But why did she still have to be so damn beautiful?

Finally she nodded. "I'll be home if you need anything."

"I won't," Emma said. When Shelby very reluctantly turned away, Luke closed the door.

Emma was staring up at him. "I heard Mommy say I look like you."

"I can see the resemblance." Although she had her mother's dimples, the hair, eyes, shape of her face were him. He'd noticed that right away.

They stood in the living room, sizing each other up, and he felt the pressure to say something life altering to his nine-year-old daughter. His flesh and blood. He should know her, know what to say to her. He should feel close to her, love her. But he felt only nervous with a stranger, a small human he was seeing for the second time. And Shelby had done this to him.

Anger churned through him but he had to tamp it down. He was the grown-up in the room even though he didn't feel like adulting today. He felt like a bull in a ballerina class.

Pull it together, McCoy, he told himself. For crying out loud, he was a detective and had faced down bad guys. It's what he did. Surely he could manage a kid.

"You want something to drink?" he asked.

"Can I have soda?" She looked hopeful.

Luke had a feeling she wasn't allowed to drink it and approved. It had a lot of calories and negligible hydration. Although technically it didn't matter in this situation because… "I don't have any."

"What do you have?" she asked.

"Come to think of it… Just water and beer."

"I'm too little for beer," she told him seriously.

"Yeah. That's the rumor."

"I'll take water."

"Good choice." He pointed to the back of the house. "Kitchen is that way."

"I know. It's like my house." Curiously she looked around his living room, frowning at the packing boxes. "But we have furniture. Grammy wouldn't like boxes all over like this."

Pam Richards didn't like much, he thought. Including him. "You can sit on one of those stools by the island."

"Okay." She climbed up and watched him fill a glass from the refrigerator's filtered water dispenser.

He set it in front of her. "You hungry?"

She shrugged. "Are you mad that you're my dad?"

Wow. That was direct. And complicated. "No. Why do you ask? Do I look mad?"

"Sorta." She studied him. "Would it be better if I was a boy?"

"No." He debated whether or not to add more, then decided she was a pretty sharp little kid. If he didn't tell the truth, she would see through him anyway. "It would be better if I'd known about you before yesterday."

"Mommy said you wanted to be a soldier and serve your country while you decided what kind of job you wanted to do."

How about that? Shelby made him sound like not so much the hot mess he'd been back then. "Your mom is right about that. I was out of high school a couple of years and worked at different jobs but none of them stuck. I didn't know what I wanted to be when I grew up."

"You're a policeman now."

"Yes. I was a cop in the army and liked it. So I studied criminal justice when I got out, and joined the Huntington Hills Police Department, first in patrol and now a detective."

"What do you do?"

He couldn't tell her the nitty-gritty of his profession because it might scare her. So, he gave her the cleaned up version. "When someone does something against the law, I have to find clues, discover the facts, so we can catch whoever did it."

"And put them in jail?"

"Yes."

It occurred to him that he could put his career skills to use now. Not the arresting part, the asking questions part.

"What grade are you in?"

"Fourth."

"What's your best subject in school?" Boy he hoped she was like her mom on this one. School wasn't his bag, not until he'd studied criminal justice.

"I like reading a lot. But math is fun."

"Good." He struggled with something else to say. "What else do you like to do?"

"I play with dolls." She took a sip of water.

"Okay." He should have expected that. But why would he? What he knew about kids, especially girls, would fit on the head of a pin. "What else?"

"Mom, Grammy and I go get pedicures together sometimes. I like that."

Nope, that wasn't in his wheelhouse either. In the shared interests category he was 0 for 2. "That sounds fun."

"It is. I get to pick out any color I want, even if it hurts Mommy's eyes."

Sounding better. "What hurts her eyes?"

"'Gargantuan Green.' It looks like slime."

"Wow." He was so out of his depth. Now what? Women liked compliments. She wasn't a woman yet but saying something nice had to be good, right? "Your hair looks nice like that."

"Thank you," she answered politely. "It's a French braid. Mommy did it like this because I wanted to look my best to meet you."

So, Emma was nervous about this, too. He should have guessed that. "Well, it worked. You look beautiful."

"Thanks." She smiled shyly. "Are you all grown up now?"

That one was from left field, but he could go with it. "I suppose so. Why do you ask?"

"Well…" She was thoughtful. "I didn't think Grammy liked you but she said it wasn't that. You just had a lot of growing up to do in the army."

He couldn't say Pam was wrong, except the part about not liking him. She hated his guts, but was clearly an important part of this child's life. Keeping that in mind was a good thing to do. "I did have to grow up. But I really wish I'd known about you."

"Yeah." She looked wistful. "Mommy said you had to go away and she thought it would be easier if you didn't have to worry about things at home."

Emma went on about Buster the dog and her

friend who worried about him when she was gone. Luke was fuming because Shelby made herself sound like Mother Teresa. The bottom line was that she should have told him she was having his baby. For her own selfish reasons she'd kept that information from him. It was a betrayal, pure and simple.

"Are you hungry now?" he asked.

"Yes." That was decisive.

"I have peanut butter and jelly." All kids liked that, right?

"Mommy told me to make sure I tell you that I'm allergic to peanuts," she said.

"Well, damn—I mean darn. Sorry."

"It's okay. Mommy says it sometimes, too."

She hadn't years ago. But back to his current problem. "What happens when you eat peanuts?"

"I get hives."

"Okay, then. No peanut butter." He went through his small inventory of food on hand: beer, frozen chicken wings, jalapeño poppers. Guy food. No fruit. Nothing healthy.

"So, what kind of food are you not allergic to?"

She got a gleam in her eyes that had mischief written all over it. "Chicken nuggets and French fries. And soda."

A little schemer. Was it wrong to admire her cleverness at the same time he disapproved of her being devious? A question for another time. "Okay, then, we'll go get some."

"Mommy won't like it," she warned.

Welcome to his world, he thought. There was a whole lot he didn't like. "I'll handle your mom."

In fact going toe-to-toe with Shelby over this might give him a little bit of payback satisfaction. He just hoped the next time they were face-to-face the urge to kiss her would be gone.

Chapter Three

Less than twenty-four hours after Emma's first visit with her father Shelby was at work and preoccupied with the consequences. Luke was all her daughter could talk about. He got her fast food and soda and Shelby was the Wicked Witch of the West who made her go to bed at—gasp—bedtime. Now she was having lunch in the teachers' lounge. She didn't feel very social or have much of an appetite but her colleagues at the other tables were wolfing down food and chattering away.

"Hey, Richards. What's up?" Brett Kamp took the chair beside hers at the otherwise empty table. He was the chairman of the math department at the high school, her boss and her friend.

"Hi." She pulled her ham on whole grain sandwich out of the ziplock bag and took a bite. It tasted like chalk.

Brett had a tuna on rye, an apple and a small individual bag of chips arranged neatly in front of him, like the components of a complicated equation. His sandwich was cut diagonally. Two triangles. And she would bet they were isosceles—with two sides of equal length. Nerds of a feather and all that.

He started eating and after swallowing a bite said, "How was your weekend?"

Nuclear Armageddon and how was yours? she wanted to say. Instead she opted for, "I've had better."

"Something up with Emma?"

"She's fine."

If you didn't count the fact that she thought her father was the coolest thing since soccer shin guards. What kid wouldn't when they got their dream junk food meal for lunch and a brand-new soccer ball? Of course he was using retail bribery and her favorite fast food to buy his daughter's affection. Shelby understood that on some level. But did he know the calorie and fat content of that stuff? It wasn't good for Emma. Did he think about that?

Probably not. But look at him. She had trouble not staring and there might be a little drooling involved. His shoulders were broad. His stomach was flat. There was probably a six-pack underneath that army strong T-shirt. And his legs looked muscular and strong. His body was in excellent shape and he'd filled out fantastically since he left. Just thinking about him made her warm.

"You okay, Shel?"

She glanced at Brett who had a questioning expression on his face. He was divorced. A nice-looking man in his thirties, trim and not as tall or exciting as Luke. And since when did she compare men to the guy who broke her heart?

"Hmm?"

"Is something wrong?" he asked.

"No. Why?"

"You're quiet today."

"It's all good." She took a big bite of her sandwich to prove it. "What's up with you?"

"I've found a volunteer to tutor in the math department," he said.

"Great. Who?"

"A friend of mine from high school, even though we always competed for math glory back then. Gabriel Blackburne. He's a business guy. Turns around underperforming companies. After working all over the country he's back in Huntington Hills to help his aunt turn around the matchmaking business she bought."

Shelby let him natter on, grateful she didn't have to contribute to the conversation. Then she realized he'd stopped talking and was staring at her.

"What?"

"Something is wrong. Don't deny it. I've known

you for quite a while now and math people learn to look for patterns. Quiet and distracted isn't yours. So give it up. What's bothering you?" He must have seen something in her face because he added, "We're friends. Don't tell me it's nothing."

She blew out a long breath. "Okay. Maybe it would help to talk."

"Can't hurt."

"This could. But a different perspective might be helpful. You're a guy."

"Yeah." His eyes narrowed nervously. "Why is that relevant?"

"I have a hypothetical question for you."

"I already don't like this conversation." He held up a hand when she started to protest. "It was my idea. Shoot."

She could see him bracing for it. "How would you feel if a woman had your baby and didn't tell you?"

His eyes widened. Clearly the question was not what he'd expected. "I'd want to know more details. About why she kept that information from me."

"Just answer the question."

"Okay." He thought for a moment. "I guess the guy's reaction would depend on his circumstances when he found out."

That surprised Shelby. She was sure he would go with male outrage about being kept in the dark. "What circumstances would those be?"

"Well, I'm divorced and don't have kids. So I fall on the single scale now. But there was a time when

I was happily married. If I'd found out that I had a child my reaction would be different."

"How so?"

"A happily married man is committed to his wife, and children if there are any. He'd be protective of them. He would go straight on the offensive, in terms of what does this person want from him?"

"What if it wasn't the woman's idea to tell him?" Emma had taken that decision out of Shelby's hands.

Brett shook his head. "Doesn't matter. All he's thinking about is his family unit being attacked."

"And if the guy isn't married?" Luke was apparently single. And now she was the one bracing herself.

"In that case he would be better able to respond in a selfless way. There wouldn't be the distraction of a wife. And if he was divorced with kids, the unit is already fractured. The revelation of a child isn't going to damage a relationship that's already broken beyond repair. He's committed to the kids he already has and it would be his job to help them be inclusive of another one."

"He doesn't have a wife or kids," she said absently.

"Shel, what's going on? This must be about Emma's father." His blue eyes brimmed with sympathy and curiosity. "You never talked about him and I didn't ask. It's none of my business. But you're obviously going through something now. Maybe I can help."

She put her sandwich down and met his gaze. "I was seventeen and had been forbidden to see him. Luke McCoy. He lived next door and was a rebel."

"Yeah. I know the type," he said.

"My mother didn't like him."

He winced. "You know as well as I do that just makes the situation even more tempting to a teenager."

"Yeah. A temptation I couldn't resist." The feelings had been so big. Even now when she looked at him she could remember them. "That was the only time I disobeyed my mother. It didn't go well."

He nodded. "We see that here every day. Kids hook up, break up and it's the end of the world," he said. "From our perspective as adults, we know life does go on."

"And for me it went on as a pregnant teenager who had to finish high school." She couldn't quite meet his gaze for this part. "He broke up with me. Right after that I found out I was pregnant and told my mother right away. I was scared and she was all I had. She made me promise not to tell him because she believed that he would ruin my life. I kept that promise—until Luke contacted me and wanted to talk."

"What happened?"

"I made up my mind I was going to tell him. Disobey my mother again. But before I could he said he'd joined the army."

"So you kept quiet," Brett guessed.

Shelby nodded. "And he left not knowing the truth."

"So why is it an issue now?"

"He's back. Next door. His mother moved to Phoenix and he has to fix up her house to get it ready to sell."

"I see."

"The timing is interesting in a way. Naively I'd hoped Emma wouldn't start asking questions about her father. But she has been."

Brett took a chip from the small bag and chewed it thoughtfully. "There are people who believe men have a right to know about their offspring. That it's the moral and decent thing to do."

"So you think I'm immoral and indecent?"

"Not what I said, Richards." He met her gaze. "Some men don't want to know. They don't want the emotional or financial responsibility. In those cases the woman has to go after him for child support."

"I never wanted anything. When I didn't tell him I knew she'd be mine alone to take care of in every way." But something in his tone made her ask, "Would you want to know?"

"Yes," he said immediately.

"So you're saying I should have told him?"

"Does it matter what I think?"

"No. The damage is already done." She explained to him about Emma overhearing, then marching next door to confront Luke.

Brett whistled in surprise. "Gotta love that kid. She meets life head-on."

"I know. Luke is like that. And it made his teenage years—" She thought a moment, searching for the right word. "Turbulent. I'm not looking forward to that stage with Emma."

"So, look on the bright side."

She shook her head. "I'm not seeing one right now."

"You're so glass half-empty, Richards." He smiled. "Now that she knows about him and he wants to be in her life, you have someone else to help you parent her. A man's perspective. Or should I say, a father's perspective."

She smiled for the first time. "Well aren't you the glass half-full guy today."

"That's me. Rainbows and unicorns."

"Ha. Unicorns are a myth. And rainbows are caused by refraction and dispersion of light in water droplets making a spectrum of—"

"What a buzzkill you are." He laughed. "No wonder I'm the favorite math teacher at Huntington Hills High School."

"Numbers are easy. You can count on them. No pun intended. But life is hard."

And currently hers was impossible. How could she co-parent when Luke hated her with the passion of a thousand suns?

Luke was feeling pretty proud of himself. For his second visit with Emma, Shelby had put him on the list of people authorized to pick her up from school. Since he had the day off, he was going to do that. This time she was staying at his house for dinner and he had kid-friendly, nonallergenic food in the refrigerator—frozen nuggets and fries. The only thing that could trip him up was how to entertain her until then.

Shelby had told him to ask about homework. In the after-school program Emma attended they usually did that first and then activities. But his philosophy was that she'd been in a classroom all day and needed to let off a little steam before tackling books. And he thought he had just the thing for an activity.

Now he was outside of Emma's classroom waiting for her to be dismissed. There were a few moms, too, and they were giving him funny looks. In this era of know your surroundings, see something/say something, he understood it was their duty. But it made him want to flash his badge and ID and assure them he was one of the good guys. He thought better of it, however, not wanting to make this particular first with his daughter weird.

Thankfully the bell rang, her classroom door opened and an older woman who must be the teacher stood there. He could see a line of kids not very patiently waiting just inside for the signal to move out.

Finally the teacher said, "You're dismissed, children. Remember, no running."

The first few filed outside and some went with the waiting moms. A couple of others managed to maintain decorum until getting to the open playground before disobeying the order not to run. Then Emma walked outside. She saw him and suddenly looked shy and uncomfortable. How long would it be until she just smiled as if he'd been around forever? Like the other kids did with their parents. He wouldn't have to wonder about it if he'd known from the beginning.

Emma walked over to him. "Hi. You're here."

"Didn't your mom tell you I would be?"

"Yeah. It's just—"

Emma's teacher walked over. "Hi. I'm Audrey Lambert, Emma's teacher."

"Luke McCoy," he said and shook her hand. "I'm Emma's dad." This time he did pull out his ID and badge then let her examine them.

"Thank you." She handed them back. "It's nice to meet you."

"Same here."

This woman smiled as if a long-lost dad showed up there every day. "Shelby called and said you'd be picking Emma up."

"Yes. I'm an HHPD detective so my schedule isn't nine to five, off on weekends. With days off during the week I can fill in, give Emma a break from routine."

"I'm sure she'll enjoy that."

Luke was about to find out. "I don't want to take up too much of your time so we'll get going."

She smiled at the little girl. "I'll see you tomorrow."

"Okay. Bye, Mrs. Lambert." Emma looked really uncomfortable.

Luke walked beside her on the way to his truck

and wondered if her pink backpack was heavy. He pointed to it. "Can I take that for you?"

"No."

Was it independence or something else? This wasn't the same kid who'd chowed down on junk food and got excited about a new soccer ball. This felt like going backward with her and he wasn't sure what he'd done.

When they got to the lot where he'd parked, Luke opened the rear passenger door. "Back seat, kid. In the middle, remember? Like when we went for fast food. It's the safest place."

"But, Mommy—"

"It's not negotiable." On patrol he'd seen too many accidents where things ended badly because someone thought it would be okay just this once.

She settled in to his satisfaction, but didn't look happy. Luke got behind the wheel and started the engine, then backed out of the space. He made a right turn out of the parking lot.

"This isn't the way home," Emma said.

"We're going to make a stop first."

"Where?" There was suspicion all over that single word.

"It's a surprise."

"But Mommy always wants me to do homework first."

"Today is going to be a little bit different. Is that all right?" he asked.

"She'll be mad."

He glanced in the rearview mirror and saw her frowning uncertainly as she looked out the window. It hit him that this was only the second time he'd ever had a child in his truck. This wasn't just any child either. This was his daughter. He had a kid. Right now he didn't much care if her mother was mad about a change in routing. And speaking of mad, at some point he was going to have to break this news to his mother. That was going to be fun. Not.

When they got closer to the final destination, Emma asked, "Are we going to the park?"

"Good eye. We definitely are. You're pretty smart."

"Why?" Again with the suspicion.

"Can you guess?"

"To play soccer," she said.

"What was your first clue?"

"There's a soccer ball back here."

"You're a pretty good detective."

"Not really."

He glanced in the rearview mirror again and saw that she wasn't smiling. He'd thought she would but maybe when they got there and played ball she'd perk up.

Minutes later he parked in the lot and slid out of the truck before opening the rear passenger door. After lifting Emma out, he grabbed the ball and headed for a wide-open grassy area.

"This looks good to me. What do you think?" he asked.

"It's okay, I guess."

"I used to play when I was a kid, but I'm pretty rusty now." Luke dropped the ball at his feet and nudged it in her direction. "Kick it back to me."

She did but there was very little enthusiasm.

"Let's do it again until I get the hang of it." He nudged it back to her with a little more oomph.

"Okay." She trapped the ball with one foot then sent it back half-heartedly.

For a few minutes they kicked it back and forth in silence. He knew she was a striker on her team, which meant she was passed the ball and her job was to try and score a goal. He was a rookie at this dad thing but he'd have to be blind not to see she wasn't enjoying this. Winning points with her was the objective and he'd expected a soccer day to be a slam dunk. And yes, he was mixing his sports metaphors.

"Is something on your mind?" he asked.

"No. It's fine." But her tone said that wasn't even in the same ballpark as the truth.

"What's bugging you?"

She shrugged, then kicked the ball back. "Nothing."

"Look, kid, I'm a detective. It's my job to read people. So out with it. What's bothering you?"

"You'll get mad," she said.

"I won't. Promise." And if he did she would never know.

"Okay." She caught her bottom lip between her

teeth. Something her mom always did. "I don't know what to call you."

"My name is Luke."

"I know. But Mommy says not to call adults by their first names." She rubbed a finger underneath her nose then skipped to her right to stop the ball. "But you're my father."

She was so serious and he wanted to lighten the mood. "I think calling me 'father' is a little too formal. Don't you?"

She shrugged and there wasn't a flicker of a smile. "I guess. It sounds kinda weird."

"Yeah." And yet another issue that could have been avoided if only he'd known about her. "How does 'Dad' sound?"

She shrugged again, obviously a favorite communication device for her because this time it was a big movement of her shoulders. There was a noticeable lack of verbal accompaniment.

"How about this?" He thought for a moment. "I'll answer to Luke, or Dad, but not doofus, knucklehead or Pop. You decide. Deal?"

"Okay."

It was affirmative if not heartfelt. Now what? "So, Emma, why don't you show me how to dribble, pass and shoot."

She picked up the ball he just kicked back to her. "Can I go home now?"

"I thought you loved to play soccer." This was beginning to land somewhere in the vicinity of epic fail.

"I need to do homework."

And she was tired, hungry and thirsty, at least that's what she claimed. He wasn't going to force this so they headed back to the truck. She insisted on carrying the ball. Apparently the coach stressed responsibility for equipment. But in this case that turned out to be bad.

One minute she was walking along, the next the ball slipped out of her hands and rolled over the sidewalk and curb into the parking lot. She went racing after it before he could stop her.

"Emma, wait."

But either she didn't hear him or chose to ignore the warning because she kept going and tripped on the cement. There was no sound for several seconds and he swore his heart stopped.

He went down on one knee and helped her sit up. "Are you okay?"

She took one look at the blood on her leg and the rip in her jeans and started to cry. "I want Mommy."

Luke would never admit it but right that second he wanted Shelby, too. He was conflicted about whether to strangle her or plead for help but right this second he was the last line of defense. He picked Emma up in his arms and set her in the back seat before buckling her in. Then he retrieved the soccer ball which miraculously escaped being run over by a car. On the way back to the house he called Shelby who was home from work and gave her a quick account of what happened. She assured him she'd be waiting for them.

Sure enough she was outside when he parked in his driveway. He stopped the truck and turned off the engine, then jumped out and met her by the rear door.

"What should I do?" he demanded.

"Take a breath. I'll just clean it up." When he opened the truck door she said to Emma, "Hey, sweetie, unbuckle your seat belt and come inside so I can—"

"No, Mom. I can't walk. It really hurts."

The tears and hostile look she gave him were like a knife in his chest and the need to fix this bordered on desperation. "I'll carry her."

Shelby looked at him then nodded. "Okay. There's a bathroom downstairs—"

"I know. Same floor plan."

She nodded then led the way inside as Luke scooped the crying child into his arms and carried her. The bathroom was down the hall to the left and he took her there, nudging the light on with his elbow before setting her on the countertop by the sink. Shelby walked in with a pair of scissors.

"Sweetie, I'm going to cut off the leg of your pants."

"You can't, Mommy." Emma gave Luke a look that said this was all his fault. "These are my favorite jeans."

"And now they'll be your favorite cutoffs." Shelby's reassuring smile was also sympathetic. "They're ruined, honey. I know the style is to have rips in your pants, but not like this. After today they'll be cut-off shorts."

Emma rubbed her sweatshirt-clad arm under her nose and sniffled, but didn't say anything. Talking the whole time, explaining what she was doing, Shelby gently washed the scraped knee with soap and water then poured peroxide over it. She dabbed around the edges before blowing gently on the bubbling disinfectant. When it was dry enough, she put antibiotic ointment on an adhesive strip and secured it over the wound.

"Good as new," she pronounced. "You're all set to go over to your father's house—"

Tears gathered in Emma's eyes as she looked at her mom. "I don't want to."

"But you're supposed to have dinner there," Shelby said.

"I want to stay home now."

Shelby started to push back but Luke held up a hand. "It's okay. We'll do it another time." He looked at Emma. "I'm sorry about your knee."

She sniffled but didn't say anything.

He nodded. "Okay, then. Talk to you later."

He walked through the house and outside. Just as he was unlocking his front door he heard Shelby call his name. He whirled to look at her. "Is she okay?"

"Fine. She just remembered she left her backpack in your truck. And she didn't do her homework because she was at the park."

"Oh. Right." He refused to feel guilty about that. "I'll get it."

Shelby followed him down the path to the driveway. "Luke, accidents happen. Don't beat yourself up over it."

"How do you know I am?" He retrieved Emma's pink backpack from the truck's rear seat and handed it over.

"I just do," she said.

Like she knew him. He wasn't that guy anymore. "I'm a former soldier and now a cop. I protect and serve. This was my watch and she got hurt."

"You're not perfect and neither am I. Stuff happens. We deal with it."

"You knew just what to say. I didn't."

"You'll learn. Just be there," she advised.

"What does that mean?"

"It means that in my experience you weren't there. You and I had a rough patch and you called it quits. I don't even know why you bothered to tell me you'd joined the army."

"I thought you should know. And I definitely should have known about Emma."

"If I had told you would it have made a difference? You still had to go." Her eyes were flashing now, more green than brown. "You had to do that and I had to do what I needed to for me and Emma. Be honest with me and yourself. Wasn't it easier to go and do what you had to without knowing?"

Luke didn't know what to say. As it turned out

he didn't need to say anything because she didn't wait for an answer. She turned and walked away from him. Independent. He could see where Emma got it. Why in blazes did that strike him as being sexy as hell?

Chapter Four

Emma was asleep and her grandmother was downstairs watching TV so the house was quiet while Shelby sat at the desk in her bedroom and corrected math tests. She was having trouble concentrating. The smoldering look of anger in Luke's eyes kept popping into her mind. She was beginning to recognize it as a clue that something hadn't gone well on a visit with his daughter. Not her finest moment but she experienced the tiniest bit of satisfaction because he'd arrogantly refused any input from her. Then the voice of guilt reminded her he wouldn't need input if she'd told him in the first place.

He always had been stubborn. And too good-looking.

She wished the years hadn't been kind to him but that wasn't the case. Whatever he'd experienced had made him even better looking than the bad boy she remembered. That increased his sexiness quotient by a factor of ten.

She finally finished grading the test it had taken her far too long to do. When she realized it was a failing grade, she sighed. This kid was doing everything right—homework, extra credit—and just wasn't getting it. Maybe Brett's friend, the volunteer math tutor, could help. She made a note to talk to her supervisor about it tomorrow.

Her cell phone vibrated and she automatically glanced at the screen. Her heart skipped a beat when she saw it was a text from Luke. She wanted to ignore it because he was probably just venting more anger at her. That increased her guilt quotient by a factor of ten. She was tired but she owed him and picked up her phone to read the message.

Need to talk.

It's late. Tomorrow? She hit Send.

His answer came back almost immediately. It can't wait. Coming over.

No!! Mom still up!!

Shelby waited for his response but it didn't come and she sighed. Rejection shouldn't be a surprise. He already hated and resented her. Nothing was going to change that. There was no reason to feel bad just because she didn't ask "how high" when he said jump. This situation was still new and things had to be worked out.

A soft tapping on her bedroom window made her jump. She looked over and gasped when she saw Luke there. Ten years ago he used to squeeze through a loose board in the fence separating the houses. Somehow he would climb up on the back patio cover and she would open the window for him to sneak inside. It had been thrilling then. If she was honest it was still thrilling now, in an "I wonder how he's going to chew me out now" kind of way.

She went to the window, slid the pane to the side and he climbed through the opening. Why did she have to notice that his shoulders were broader and didn't fit through quite as easily now?

"Where is the screen?" Of all the things she could have said that's what she came up with?

"I'll put it back."

"What's so gosh darn important that it couldn't wait until tomorrow?"

"You walked away earlier. I wasn't finished talking."

"Tough, I was. And Emma was upset. I needed to get back to her. You and I were just talking in circles."

He dragged his fingers through his thick, dark hair. "I'm just trying to understand."

"Good luck with that."

"What does that mean?"

"There are no words that will help. Until you're a pregnant seventeen-year-old girl who was dumped by her boyfriend, who then for some mysterious reason thinks he needs to announce that he joined the army and had to go, you will never understand why I made the decision I did."

"Look, Shelby—"

"No, Luke. You look." There was a foot between them and he was a lot taller but something inside her finally snapped. "I told you how sorry I am and sincerely mean that. If I could change it, somehow make it better, I would. But I can't. And I won't say it again." She blew out a breath. "Emma will see you tomorrow as arranged. Now get out of my room."

Luke ignored her and sat on her queen-sized bed. "Tell me again."

Did he not hear what she just said? "What?"

"You said you were going to disobey your mother and tell me. But you didn't. I want to hear it one more time."

She shook her head and wanted to refuse. But this was the least she could do. "I was young. Terrified. And whether you believe me or not, the truth is that I didn't want to ruin your life." She turned the desk chair to face him and sat down on the edge. "My parents were divorced. My dad cheated on my mom then married the woman and had another family."

His mouth pulled tight for a moment. "I remember."

"All I had was my mom."

"And she had no use for me." His soft tone didn't take the bitterness out of the words.

"Look at it from her perspective. You got in trouble more than once. If it wasn't for your dad's cop friend Lou Murphy, you'd have been in even more serious trouble. That gave you a reputation. And a couple of criminal justice classes in community college wasn't a career path in my mother's view. You were struggling and she was afraid I would get caught up in that struggle. In a bad way."

His eyes flickered and for just a moment it looked as if her words got through to him. Then the anger was back, maybe a bit less intense. "She never gave me a chance."

"I did. And you turned your back as if I didn't exist."

"I wrote you letters. I told you that."

"And I told you I didn't get them. I thought you walked away without a backward glance." Her hands were shaking so she folded them in her lap. "I didn't have a lot of choices. In fact there were two. Live on the street—pregnant and alone. Or agree to my mom's terms and not tell you I was going to have a baby."

Luke stared at the math papers on the desk behind her. "So you're a high school math teacher. Looks like the choice you made worked out well for you. Your mom must be proud."

She noted the sarcasm in his voice but didn't

flinch. Not anymore. "I would make a different choice today."

"You and your mother stole nine years of my daughter's life from me," he said, just a little too loud.

"Shh." She put her finger to her lips and something darkened in his eyes. "My mother's priority was protecting me. Mine is protecting Emma."

"I wouldn't hurt her."

"That's what you promised me and yet you did." She refused to look away. She was over defending herself. Sorry would never be enough. "Kids need routine. After school, homework gets done first and then she does whatever she wants. She's learned to follow the rules."

"Like you?" Suddenly the fight seemed to go out of him and he shook his head. "Look, this is pointless."

"I agree. That's why I walked away earlier," she reminded him.

"Nothing you say can make it right."

"I know that." She sighed as the fight went out of her, too. "So what in the world was important enough that you climbed up and came through my window?"

"Emma is that important. I want to be a father to my daughter."

"I'm not stopping you."

"I know." He looked down for a moment. "But I didn't get to grow into this role gracefully like you did."

Hearing that truth had her on the verge of apologizing yet again but she held back. If she said it a million times it wouldn't dissolve his resentment. "You're not wrong about that. But I still don't know why you're here."

"It kills me to ask you for anything. And if you say 'I told you so'—"

"I can't promise not to do that, so just spit it out, Luke."

"You owe me."

"Okay. So what do you want?"

He stood and paced, then stopped in front of her and looked down. "If your offer still stands to be a go-between with Emma and me, I'd like to take you up on it."

This was unexpected. "Of course I'll help. For Emma," she added. "But I thought everything was going well. That you bought your way in with fast food and a soccer ball. Also a day at the park without making her do homework first probably bought you some credit."

"Don't judge." One corner of his mouth curved up for a moment before he turned serious again. "She's different with you. Carefree. Happy. With me she's quiet, tense, guarded. I want what you have."

"I get it."

"I've already lost so much." There was an edge in his voice. "She doesn't even know what to call me."

"What did you tell her?"

"That I'd answer to Luke, Dad and almost anything except doofus or Pop."

"That's a good response."

"Yeah?"

"Absolutely. Humor and honesty. It will just take time."

He nodded. "I think with you there she'd relax and be more comfortable. If you accept me, she will."

Shelby had accepted him before and had her heart handed back to her. That's not what he was talking about but she went there anyway. Just as a reminder to keep her eye on the goal.

"Okay. I'm happy to help. On one condition."

His eyes narrowed. "And that is?"

"You have to act as if you're not mad at me. Kids notice everything and it won't help you win her trust if she sees how you feel."

He thought about that. "I'll do my best."

"Okay then." For just a second she flashed back to a time when he'd been with her in this room and they couldn't keep their hands off each other. "You know if things had gone differently, we might be married."

The idea popped into her head but she couldn't believe she'd said it out loud. Apparently the man still made her mind turn to mush.

Luke stared at her, looking more startled than anything. But, oddly, there was no anger. "Yeah. I'd say we dodged a bullet."

"Definitely."

He moved toward the open window. "So, we'll come up with a plan. How we're going to work together. Just so we're clear, this isn't personal."

"Of course." She wondered why he felt the need to spell that out.

"Being a dad to Emma has to be my focus."

"Why don't we both come up with a list of ideas, things to do with her, and pick a few. See how it goes."

"Okay." He went back out the window. "I'll be in touch."

He replaced the screen and then he was gone. He was right, she thought. They had no connection anymore other than Emma. But how she wished that he didn't have to pretend not to be mad at her. She wished he could forgive her. And if it wasn't asking too much, she super wished that she could stop thinking about how hot and handsome he was.

But she was wishing for the moon on every count.

"You've been staring at your computer screen for five minutes and haven't typed in a thing. At this rate we'll be here all night."

Luke looked at the man facing him in the Huntington Hills Police Department squad room across the two desks pushed up against each other. Lou Murphy, the detective he'd been partnered with, was staring back at him. The older man had known his dad and took Luke under his wing after the accident that killed his father. The guy looked like a gray-haired basset hound with his sad, droopy brown eyes. Hell of a good cop and Luke was lucky to be his partner, luckier still to be his friend.

But the qualities that made him a top-notch detective told him something wasn't right with Luke. He wouldn't be able to blow this off.

Luke looked around the busy room. There were officers in khaki uniforms with handcuffed suspects. Plainclothes detectives and clerical employees were answering phones. But for the moment he and Murph were clear.

"You got a couple minutes for a coffee break?" he asked the other man.

"Yeah." Murph stood and headed to the break room where a pot of the world's worst coffee was located. "I'll buy."

That was his running joke. Everyone pitched in to share the cost of supplies. Unfortunately no one knew how to make a really good cup of coffee. Luke followed his mentor, friend and partner down the hall and into the empty room. He shut the door behind him.

There was a cheap and cheesy little wooden table in the middle of the space, a few cupboards around the perimeter. A sink, small refrigerator and a drip coffee maker on the cracked laminate countertop. The pot was half-full and Murph poured two cups.

He handed one over. "So, what's up? Problems with your mom's house?"

"Only where it's located." Luke took a sip of the hot liquid and apologized to his stomach. It tasted like battery acid.

Murph leaned back against the cupboard. "There's nothing wrong with that neighborhood."

"Not the area, just the neighbors." He might as well spill his guts. This guy would know if he was holding back. He really hoped he didn't regret not doing that. "Shelby is there. Living with her mom."

"Shelby?" The other man frowned. "Isn't that the girl you broke up with and then got drunk and disorderly over?"

"Yeah." Too late. He was already regretting saying anything.

"You were a mess, kid. Going in the army was good for you. I knew it would be when I suggested it." He took a sip of his coffee and made a face. "You're welcome for that, by the way."

"I saw her one more time before I left for basic training."

"To say goodbye," Murph guessed.

"Yeah. I thought I owed it to her to let her know."

"Okay." The man nodded thoughtfully. "So, have you seen her since you moved back into the house?"

"Yeah." He stared into the black circle of his coffee.

"And?"

"And she looks great."

"I'm not seeing the problem." His partner's expression was the one he wore when the facts and narrative didn't match. "Is she married?"

"No."

"Maybe you two could rekindle the flame—"

"Not a chance," Luke said.

"Why? Could be the fact that you're both single is a sign that—"

"It's not. Since when are you Murph the matchmaker?"

The other man grinned. "Just saying… I remember it hit you pretty hard. The breakup. Why did you do it anyway?"

"Her mother hated me. We were sneaking around and Shelby wouldn't disobey her and see me openly." She was a rule follower then and was raising Emma to be one now. "That got to me and I didn't like what it was doing to her. If she'd been seeing someone different, someone better, she could have been up front about it. She deserved that. So I told her it was best if we didn't see each other anymore." And almost immediately he'd regretted the words. But he didn't take them back. The next time he saw her was with another guy who picked her up at her house for a date. That was the night Luke got drunk. Fortunately it was Murph who arrested him.

"Surely her mom doesn't still feel that way."

"Yeah. She does." Probably even more than she did then.

"But you're not kids anymore," his friend said. "Shouldn't her daughter decide—"

"Let it go, Murph. It's not going to happen." Luke could see him getting ready to protest and he knew how to stop it. "Shelby was pregnant. She knew the last time I saw her that she was going to have my baby and didn't say a word."

He didn't often see his friend shocked speechless, but he was now. Luke filled in the silence. "I have a daughter. Emma. She's nine years old and over-heard Shelby and her mom talking about me being her father and she came over to ask me straight-out."

"Well, I'll be…"

Luke smiled at the memory of his daughter standing there on his doorstep. Since that day when he bought her fast food, she hadn't shown as much spirit and was pretty subdued. He couldn't say for sure but had a feeling that was out of character for her.

"Luke, man, I'm sorry."

"It's not your fault."

"If I hadn't mentioned the army and what it could do for you, things might have been different. But I could see you needed something." The basset hound eyes were amped up to full power. "If you hadn't gone, you'd have known about Emma—"

"Don't. That will make you crazy. Trust me, I know." Luke took a sip of the now-cold coffee. "You didn't push me into anything. No one could tell me what to do. You know that better than anyone."

"You were a stubborn son of a gun," the other man agreed.

"If it hadn't felt right, I wouldn't have enlisted." Luke remembered that time and all the reasons his decision had made so much sense. "My mom was glad I was leaving. She always blamed me for the accident. If not for me, my dad would still be here."

"It wasn't your fault, Luke. The other driver was speeding and ran a stop sign."

"Then maybe she blames me for surviving when he didn't. I don't know. But we could hardly be in the same room together without a fight." He set his mug on the table. "Now I have to tell her she has a granddaughter she didn't know about. Somehow that will be my fault, too."

"Well, for what it's worth, you have to deal with what's going on now, not the way things were then." The other man shook his head. "Why didn't Shelby tell you?"

Luke told his partner every excuse she'd given him. "Her choice was to say nothing to me about the pregnancy or be on the street."

"It could be the truth."

"Right," Luke said sarcastically. "And I'm going for a moon walk tomorrow."

"Okay. You don't believe her. But keep this in mind. You've never been a pregnant seventeen-year-old girl. And if it's true, the prospect of being thrown out of the house would be pretty scary. Just saying." Murph shrugged. "So what about now? Is she agreeable to letting you see your daughter? Assuming you want to see her."

"Of course I do. And Shelby isn't standing in the way. But Emma is a little skittish with me."

"That's to be expected. You just have to give it time."

"That's what everyone keeps telling me." And he was sick of hearing it. He wanted results. Now. Otherwise he never would have made a deal with Shelby to hang out and speed up the process. He told Murph what they'd talked about last night when he climbed through her bedroom window.

The older man looked a little skeptical. "So, let me get this straight. You agreed to spend time with this woman you don't trust in order to get to know your daughter?"

"Yeah. Why? What's wrong with that."

"I don't know." Murph rubbed a hand over his neck. "I just think you could do it on your own."

"You haven't seen the way Emma looks at me. Like I'm a stranger and she's ready to split." He wondered if he looked at Shelby that way because Murph was right. He didn't trust her and never would.

"Okay. Has Shelby brought up child support?"

"No. She hasn't mentioned it." And Luke hadn't thought about that. He should have, but the fact was that Shelby hadn't asked him for anything. In the context of their new arrangement she'd asked only that he act as if he wasn't mad at her.

"Okay, I can see why you've been so distracted. It's not every day a guy finds out he has a daughter."

"Something he should have found out nine years ago," Luke reminded him.

"That was then. This is now. Bottom line is that you have to figure out how to get along with her. For Emma's sake."

"Yeah."

"Good luck with that."

"Seriously? That's the best you can do?" Luke asked.

"Pretty much." Murph gave him a sympathetic look. "Wish I had some magic words, but I don't. Just remember that you're doing it for Emma."

"I'll try."

What he didn't mention to his partner was that part of him was looking forward a little bit to seeing Shelby. Climbing through her window had brought back memories, some of the best ones he'd ever had. He hated himself for remembering, but he couldn't seem to stop.

Chapter Five

"This is going to be fun."

Shelby said the words to Emma but she didn't believe them for a second. It was Saturday. She, Luke and Emma were going to a small carnival sponsored by the local parks and recreation department every year. There were rides, enough junk food to make kids happy and games to keep them entertained. After exchanging lists of activities, she and Luke put this one at the top, mostly because it was there for two weekends, then gone.

Emma put on a pink hooded sweatshirt and frowned. "Does he have to come?"

"By 'he' I assume you're referring to your father." Her child neither confirmed nor denied. She simply glared. "Yes, your dad has to come. He's making an effort to get to know you and you should do him the same courtesy." *Making an effort to get to know you.* Those are words Shelby had never thought she would say.

Before Emma could refute that her grandmother walked from the kitchen to the entryway by the front door. "It looks like rain. Are you sure you want to go?"

"I checked the weather report. It's going to be fine," Shelby said.

On the father/daughter front the forecast was for sun and clouds with a chance of Luke making progress with Emma. Shelby's job was to be a bridge and, by God, she was going to be the best doggone bridge anyone had ever seen.

"Are you sure you don't want to stay home with me, Em?" The woman was not happy about the whole bridge thing.

"Mom, we talked about this." Shelby gave her the back off look. "We're going to have fun. Right, Emma?"

The little girl shrugged. "I have to go, Grammy."

"Okay. Give me a hug, then." Pam went down on one knee and held her granddaughter tight against her for a moment. "Stay warm. That wind is a little chilly."

Shelby grabbed her purse and jacket from the coat tree and opened the door. Luke was standing by his truck in the driveway next to theirs. "Let's go. Your dad is waiting."

That sounded so weird. *Your dad.* Shelby wondered if it would ever feel normal. And if she felt like that it had to be even more strange for Emma. The only way to normalize the situation was to keep saying it. Let the acceptance offensive begin.

They walked across the driveway and he met them on the passenger side of the vehicle. In his battered brown leather jacket, jeans and boots he still looked every inch the heartthrob rebel he used to be.

He smiled down at his daughter. "Hi."

"Hi." Her voice was polite with a twist of 'I'm only here because she's making me do this.'

"How's your knee?" he asked.

"Gross. It's all scabby."

"It's healing," Shelby interjected, being that perky bridge over troubled waters she'd vowed to be.

"Hey." Luke's smile didn't waver when he looked at her but it also didn't reach his eyes. He was doing his best to not look mad. "Are you guys ready to do this?"

"We are," she said.

He didn't look reassured but gallantly opened the rear passenger door. "It's a long way up. Can I help you, Emma?"

"No. I can do it by myself." With an effort she climbed in and settled in the center of the back seat.

That was different. "Why are you in the middle?"

"He makes me."

"Statistics show that it's safer," he explained.

"Good to know." That was sweet, Shelby thought. Although it hadn't gotten their daughter to progress beyond male pronouns in referring to Luke.

This was their first family outing—nine years later than it should have been. And right on cue guilt smiled, waved and sat on her chest. Right now the best she could say about this was better late than never. At least when Emma was older she wouldn't have to wonder or ask questions about her dad and resent Shelby because half of her medical history was a question mark.

Luke closed the door then opened Shelby's. "Can you make it?"

"Yeah." She hauled herself up and into the front passenger seat. Very graceful and ladylike. And why on earth should she care?

Maybe because Luke was right there, his face not far from hers. His mouth not far from hers. In the old days he would have leaned in and kissed her until she was breathless and wanting. The old days were exciting. Now there was just anger and guilt. Maybe if she could help Emma accept him her guilt would ease. There was only one way to find out.

"Let's go." She forced herself to smile. It wasn't getting any easier.

Luke got behind the wheel, started the engine and put the truck in Reverse. It was a big vehicle compared to Shelby's conservative compact and he handled it with an ease that she found masculine and captivating. Sensible Shelby was starting out on this mission already at a disadvantage.

When life gives you lemons, make conversation. Continuing to be a bridge, she thought. "Emma, what do you want to ride on first?"

"I don't know."

"You like the carousel," she said.

"My favorite ride is the roller coaster." Luke glanced at her, getting where she was going with this. He took a quick look in the rearview mirror. "What's yours, Emma?"

"I don't know. I'm too little to go on most of them."

"You have to be a certain height for all the rides and last year she was too short to go on any alone." She said so that only he could hear, "She will probably need an adult to go on them this year."

"Okay."

A few minutes later he pulled the truck into the parking lot. After driving up and down rows, he finally found a spot. "Here we are."

"This is going to be fun." Maybe if she put good karma out into the universe it would smile down on this adventure.

The three of them exited the truck and headed for the entrance. Shelby tried to casually maneuver Emma between them but the little girl always ended up on the outside, holding her mother's hand. The journey of a thousand miles started with a single step, she reminded herself.

Luke paid admission and bought ride tickets before they moved through the gate and looked around. A lot of people had turned out and the three of them meandered through the crowd.

"Do you want to ride something, Emma?" Luke asked. "Maybe we should start with the carousel."

"Good idea," Shelby agreed. "We know you're tall enough for that."

"Okay." The tone had a distinct lack of enthusiasm.

There was a line so they waited their turn. It didn't take long until the three of them stepped up onto the circle with the horses that went up and down.

"Which one do you want to sit on?" Shelby asked. "There's a unicorn. You like those."

Emma's eyes lit up for the first time. "Yes, that one."

She ran to it with Luke right behind. Shelby had to remind herself to back off and let him. That was the deal. The individual horses stopped at various heights when the ride came to a halt and the unicorn was too high for Emma to get up without assistance.

"How about if I help you?" Luke said.

Emma hesitated and looked at Shelby before finally nodding. "Okay."

At nine her little girl was getting too big for Shelby to lift but Luke easily handled it. Then he buckled the belt around her to prevent her sliding off. Shelby and Luke took up positions on either side of her and after the ride operator checked that everyone was securely fastened, they started to move up and down while going in a circle, and Emma smiled as the wind blew her hair.

"Look at you, Emma. I'll get a picture." She slid her phone from her jeans pocket and held it up before pushing the button. Nothing like memorializing this child's stoic expression for all eternity. "I'll get one of you and your dad." She did and said to him, "I'll forward these to you."

"Thanks."

When the ride stopped, Emma undid the belt and slid off the unicorn before anyone could help her. That was partly about independence and partly control. So little of this situation was within her power to manage, but she was going to do what she could.

After leaving the carousel enclosure they walked around, trying to decide what to go on next. There was the Tilt-O-Whirl that rocked back and forth while the individual cars and riders turned in a circle.

Shelby pointed at it. "That one is a hard no for me."

"Why doesn't that surprise me?" Luke grinned.

She felt the full force of that smile because she hadn't seen it for ten years. Suddenly he looked like the hot guy who had stolen her heart. She tripped and he caught her arm.

"You okay?" he asked.

"Yeah. Clumsy." She pulled herself together.

"Why aren't you surprised Mommy said no?" Emma looked up at him, curious.

"Because when I rode that with her a long time ago before you were born, she got sick all over me."

"Mommy, you threw up on him?"

"She did," he told her. "After eating cotton candy. My white shirt had pink all over it."

"Eww." The little girl made a face but the story clearly caught her interest.

"It's official," Shelby said. "Humiliation is forever."

"Okay. Pass on that one." Luke pointed to a ride that had airplanes. "That might be fun."

"I want the pink plane," Emma said.

Apparently the idea of pink puke didn't put her off the color.

When they got to the ticket taker Luke started to hand over enough tickets for the three of them.

Shelby stopped him. "You two go. Only two can ride in the plane and after reliving my past, I'm not sure my stomach can handle it."

"But, Mom—"

"It's okay, peanut. I'll wait for you guys here. Go ride the pink one with your dad."

Tickets were handed over and she watched the two of them get in their plane. Luke made sure her seat belt was fastened securely. Moments later they took off and all the planes lifted at the same time while going in a circle. Then the arms holding them went up and down and she could hear her daughter's laughter.

Shelby snapped more pictures with her phone and

memories of long ago flashed through her mind. Telling her mom she was meeting friends at the carnival. Technically it wasn't a lie because Luke was a friend. And so much more then. Because she'd been forbidden to see him, every second they spent together was precious and so very exciting. And now they were here with their daughter. It made her head spin without riding anything but recollections.

Emma's cheeks were flushed when she got off the ride and ran over. "Mommy, did you see me?"

"I did. Was it fun?"

"Yes." She looked up at Luke. "He made it go up and down."

Again with the masculine pronoun. She saw the muscle in his jaw jerk as if he was clenching his teeth. She wanted to preach patience but couldn't, not with Emma listening.

The little girl pointed to a booth just ahead that was displaying stuffed animals hanging from the canvas top. "I want one of those."

They walked over and Shelby checked it out. "Those aren't for sale, sweetie. You have to win one."

One didn't have to be fluent in nine-year-old body language to see the disappointment. Apparently it was too much for Luke.

He moved closer to check it out. Cans were set up and the way to win one of the prizes was to knock down a certain number with a baseball.

"I'll give it a try," he said.

"You will?" Emma had hope again.

"Yeah. I'm not making any promises, but I played some baseball in high school."

"Your dad was the pitcher," Shelby told her.

"Were you any good?" the little girl asked.

He laughed. "Sometimes."

"Can you try?" Pleading made her brown eyes big.

"Yes. But I make no guarantees," he warned. "Try not to be disappointed."

"That's like telling her not to be surprised when a unicorn pokes that horn in her eye."

"Your motivational speech could use work," he said.

"Are you feeling the pressure?" she teased.

"Not me. Army strong."

He walked up and paid to play, which gave him six chances to knock down four small cans. After picking up a ball, Luke eyed his target, threw and knocked it over. Emma clapped her hands. Number two ball took down the next one and she jumped up and down. He missed the third one and she groaned.

"It's okay. Good try," she encouraged.

Luke looked at Shelby. "Wonder where she heard that?"

"Can't imagine," she said, teasing.

He knocked down the next can.

Emma closed her eyes and said, "I can't look."

"Me either," Luke said.

"But you have to!" Her eyes popped open. Then she giggled. "I get it. You're kidding me."

"I am." He winked. "Okay, here goes."

Completely serious now, the little girl looked up at him. "Mommy always says just do your best. It's all anyone can ever ask of you."

"Then that's what I'll do."

Shelby nodded her encouragement then she and Emma held their breath and kept very quiet for his last try. The bottle went down with a metallic clang.

"You did it!" Emma threw herself into his arms. "Did you see, Mommy? My dad did it!"

Suddenly she was looking at him as if he were her hero. Shelby saw the emotion in his face and his effort to be nonchalant. It was a big, fat failure. She could see how much this meant to him and guilt came back with a vengeance.

How would he have looked seeing his baby daughter for the first time? Or holding her tiny body in his arms. There were consequences to the decision she made and she was seeing them now. Suddenly "what if" and "if only" were her two best friends. And she didn't like them, or herself, very much.

Luke parked the truck in his driveway just as the sun was going down. Even though the chilly wind had gotten colder and stronger, Emma didn't want to leave the carnival. And he didn't want to leave her. But he'd backed Shelby's play that it was time go home and have dinner.

Still, he would always remember the look in his daughter's eyes when he won her that stuffed animal. She picked a bear and this day was the best he'd had in a very long time. And not just because of Emma. Shelby was sweet and funny, just like she'd been when he knew her before. Sometimes he actually forgot that he was supposed to be mad at her. It was impossible to keep up that level of anger, but he would never be able to trust her.

He shut off the truck's engine. "Home sweet home, ladies."

"This was the best day." Emma removed her seat belt, grabbed her new bear and squeezed between the driver and passenger seats. "I had such a good time."

"Me, too, kid." He smiled at her and she returned it.

"You should come over for dinner at our house."

Shelby had just opened her door and the overhead light revealed her surprise and hesitation. "We don't know what Grammy's cooking tonight. There might not be enough for another person."

"I know what we're having. She told me this morning not to eat too much junk so I'd have room for spaghetti and meatballs. It's my favorite." The little girl looked at him. "Do you like spaghetti?"

The innocent eagerness on her face proved she had no idea how her grandmother felt about him. To be fair, probably Pam should get points for not bad-mouthing him in front of his daughter.

"Spaghetti is one of my favorite meals," he told her.

Luke met Shelby's gaze and silently dared her to tell Emma that he wasn't welcome. He could deal with Pam. He was army strong. No doubt she didn't want him there but he would risk marching into hell itself to spend a little more time with the child he'd finally managed to impress.

Shelby looked uneasy but finally nodded. "Okay. Spaghetti it is. Let's go tell Grammy there will be one more for dinner."

"Yay!" Emma clutched the bear tight as she let herself out of the truck.

Luke followed them across the driveway and up to the front door. The porch light was on, letting them know someone was waiting. It had been a long time since anyone was at home watching for him and he felt a pang of envy mix with a pocket of loneliness.

Shelby found the house key in her purse and put it in the lock, turning it to open the door and let them inside. The smell of onion, garlic and tomato sauce filled the air.

"Hi, Mom, we're home."

When the older woman met them in the entryway the whiplash-fast change in her expression was almost comical. She went from a welcoming smile to a look that demanded to know why the spawn of Satan was in her house.

"Grammy, look!" Emma held up the bear that was half again as big as she was. "See what my dad won for me at the carnival?"

Pam wouldn't look at him and just focused on her grandchild. To her credit she managed to smile. "Look at this. Is it a girl or boy bear?"

"Boy," Emma told her. "His name is Emmet."

"Hello, Emmet." Pam took the furry, stuffed paw in her hand and shook it. "Nice to meet you."

"My dad had to knock down cans with a ball to win him for me."

Pam still wouldn't look at him. "I think this big guy is going to need his own room."

"Oh, Grammy, you're silly."

"Only with you." The older woman's smile and the warmth in her eyes showed the unconditional love she had for this child.

"It was a pretty impressive performance, Mom." Shelby's voice was a little too perky, the enthusiasm way too forced. "He was cool and collected when he took down those bottles. They were no match for his nerves of steel."

"He always had nerve." Pam met his gaze then and hers said the words were not a compliment.

"Mommy, I need to take Emmet upstairs and make room for him. Can you help me?"

Shelby took off her jacket and settled it on the coat rack along with her purse. She was stalling for time to come up with an answer. Finally she turned back and said, "Peanut, we have a guest and it would be rude to leave him alone after inviting him to dinner."

"He's not alone." Emma was completely and blissfully unaware of the tension in the adults around her. "Grammy's here."

Shelby gave him a helpless look, as if to say "that's what I'm afraid of." She bent over to look at her daughter. "You invited your father, Emma, and it's the hostess's responsibility to make sure everyone feels comfortable."

The little girl looked confused. "Grammy always makes me feel comfortable."

"It's okay." Luke nodded at Shelby, letting her know he would be fine. "You should help her settle the bear in his new home."

Her grandmother smiled tenderly at the child. "You go ahead and find a place for him, love. I'm sure Luke and I can find something to talk about."

Shelby looked as if she'd rather jump off a steep cliff, but it was either go with the flow or try to explain to this little girl why he couldn't be left alone with her grandmother. "Okay, sweetie. But we have to be quick."

"I will, Mommy."

Shelby's look said "I'm sorry about this because it won't be quick." She sent a warning glance to her mother that said "go easy." Luke was surprised that he could still read her so easily. Ten years ago, everything she felt was right there on her face, except that last time.

When they were alone, Pam said, "Can I get you a drink?"

"Am I going to need one?"

She turned away and walked into the kitchen. He followed, not wanting Emma to hear this conversation any more than her grandmother obviously did.

Pam took a bottle of scotch from the cupboard above the refrigerator and poured a small amount into a tumbler. "As I recall, you had a better than passing acquaintance with alcohol."

"I was busted for it," he admitted.

Her eyes widened in surprise for a moment. "So you admit it."

"Yeah. And I admit that I got lucky that the cop who caught me knew my dad. I was young and stupid."

She set the glass on the island between them. "So, you're older and wiser now?"

"I hope so." Two could play let's bring up past transgressions. "You threatened, bullied and intimidated Shelby into not telling me that she was pregnant with my baby."

"Yes." Her eyes were hostile and hard. "And I would do the same thing again."

"What about what Shelby wanted?"

"I did it for her."

"You manipulated her," he said.

"Wrong thing, right reason." Pam was rigid, relentless. "I would do anything to protect my child. And her child."

"From me?" He moved closer and set his hands on the granite-topped island, ignoring the untouched drink there. "You wouldn't even meet me. You didn't know me. What did you have against me?"

"I knew enough. You had a reputation all over town. Wild and unpredictable, everyone said. It was selfish of you to jeopardize Shelby. Disaster was inevitable and I didn't want her anywhere near you when it happened. She'd have been collateral damage."

There was enough truth in her words to keep him from pushing back on them. If he was being honest, it's why he joined the army when Murph brought up the possibility. Then she could find someone that she didn't have to sneak out to see. He broke up with her, for her sake. But those words would never come out of his mouth, not within hearing distance of this woman.

"You never gave me a chance," he said again.

"I didn't want you in Shelby's life. She was a straight-A honor student at the top of her class. You were older, drifting from job to job without goals. I didn't want you to keep my daughter from reaching hers." She looked away for a moment, pressing her lips together. "She had potential—then she was pregnant. So I had two lives to protect and I didn't want you mixed up in either of them."

"Even though I had a right to know?"

"I had a duty to keep you from breaking their hearts then." She glared at him. "But now you're back and will probably do it in spite of my efforts."

Luke was hotheaded by nature which was partially responsible for his youthful reputation. Gossip had inflated it but that was neither here nor there. Army discipline along with time to mature had cultivated the self-control that turned him into a good soldier and now a good cop. He wanted to push back, defend himself to her, but it would be empty words. Success was the best revenge and he would just have to show her she was wrong about him.

He met her gaze and in a calm and even voice said, "I intend to be the best father to Emma that I know how to be. You might want to let me screw up before judging."

"I have no doubt you will."

Then Emma and Shelby walked into the room. He wanted his daughter in his life which meant he was going to have to share her with the grandmother she clearly loved. Battle lines were drawn and neither of them would budge but there was silent agreement that it was between the two of them.

Pam gave no hint of their conversation as she reminded Emma her nightly chore was to set the table and remember there would be an extra plate. Shelby glanced at him, clearly curious about what happened, and he shrugged.

But he realized that the conversation with Pam was a window into Shelby's impossible situation as a pregnant teenager. He had been contractually committed to leaving, even if she'd told him about the baby. If they'd married school would have been hard and she might not have gone. Money would have been tight for a family living on army pay. School and childcare would have been hurdles along with his deployments when she'd have been alone.

But, with her mom's help, she did go to college while raising a baby. How remarkable was that? And Emma was a terrific kid. Shelby was a good mom. Would any of that have happened if he'd been in the picture?

They would never know. He just knew right this

minute that he liked her. He'd been fighting with everything he had to hang on to his resentment but the confrontation with her mother changed everything. That would make sharing their child easier but complicated the hell out of his feelings for Shelby.

Anger was easier than this growing attraction.

Chapter Six

After Luke left and Emma was asleep, Shelby pulled out the scrapbook and photo album she used to chronicle milestones from her daughter's birth to the present. She looked at a picture of herself holding her newborn baby and smiled at the memories scrolling through her mind: crawling, walking, Emma's first birthday, losing her baby teeth in the front.

Between the covers of this book were all the things Luke had missed. Shelby couldn't imagine how it would feel to be in his position. Actually, that wasn't true. If he had robbed her of the first nine years of her child's life, she would hate him with everything she had. How could he stand to even look at her?

If only she could give him back the years. That wasn't possible, but maybe it would help just a little to see Emma grow up in pictures. She glanced at the time on her phone and realized it wasn't that late. She looked out her bedroom window and saw lights on at his house.

She pulled up his cell number in her phone contacts list then tapped in U still up?

Almost immediately he answered. Yes. Why?

It's about Em. Got something to show you.

Okay.

Be right over.

His response was a big yellow thumbs-up emoji.

Shelby smiled and grabbed the album, then quietly opened her bedroom door. She went to Emma's room and peeked in to make sure she was sound asleep. The long day at the carnival must have exhausted her because she was out like a light, still clutching the bear Luke had won for her. Today was a start to their father/daughter memories so it seemed fitting to show him scenes from Emma's past to build more on.

After walking downstairs she stopped in the family room where her mom was watching a home renovation channel. "Mom? You awake?"

"Yes—" But she sat up and rubbed her eyes. She'd been dozing. "Everything okay?"

"Yeah. Emma's asleep. I was just going through this album of pictures. I thought Luke might like to see it."

The woman wasn't drowsy now. "Do you think that's a good idea?"

"If I thought it was a bad idea I wouldn't be doing it."

"Shelby, why can't you just leave this alone?"

"Because Luke is her father and he missed out on everything. It's the right thing to do."

Pam pushed a button on the side of the chair and the footrest on the recliner lowered. "Did he ask to see the pictures?"

"No. I volunteered."

"That sounds like an excuse to go over there. Please tell me you're not falling for him again."

Shelby made a scoffing sound. "That ship has sailed. He only wants a relationship with his daughter. There's no again for us, no going back."

Even if she was tempted to rekindle that spark, and she wasn't, Luke wouldn't go there. And she couldn't blame him. She had betrayed him in a very elemental way. Showing him everything she could about his daughter was all she could think of to try and make up for what she'd done.

"I won't be gone long, Mom." Before her mother could protest, Shelby turned and walked away.

Since he was just next door she didn't need a

jacket but simply hurried across the driveways and up to his door with the album pressed to her chest. She knocked and he answered almost instantly, as if he'd been watching for her.

"Hi. Come in." He pulled the door wide and stepped back to let her walk past him. "It's cold out there."

"Yeah."

She shivered, but it had less to do with the outside temperature and more to do with the man. He was wearing the same worn jeans and flannel shirt, but somehow seemed *more* everything now that they were alone.

"So, that's what you wanted to show me? An album."

"Hmm?" Oh, God. She'd been staring. Like an infatuated teen. For Pete's sake. "Yes. I'll leave it with you. Take your time going through it."

"No. You can give me context—a story to go with the pictures." His dark eyes smoldered with something that might have been anger. Or possibly a less hostile emotion. "Stay."

Her breath caught for a moment but she figured it was guilt. And that accounted for her accepting the invitation. Simple, old-fashioned guilt.

She looked around the room which was practically empty of furniture. There was a stepladder standing in the corner, plastic drop cloths, paint pans and rollers.

"Someone is getting ready to paint," she said.

"Wow, you should be the one with the detective shield."

She smiled because he was in fact teasing her. "Where do you want to look at this? There's nowhere to sit in here."

"Kitchen, I guess. We can open it on the island."

"Okay."

She followed him and set it down where he indicated, right beside a coffee mug with a dried coffee stain in the bottom. Probably from this morning, before they spent the day together.

"Can I get you anything?" he asked.

"It looks pretty bare in here. Do you actually have anything?"

"Water. Coffee. Beer."

"Tough choice." She laughed. "Not really. I'll pass."

She opened the photo album to the first page where Emma was a newborn, swaddled in a blanket and wearing a pink hat. "Look at those wide eyes and perfect little mouth. She weighed eight pounds, four ounces. Twenty inches long."

"Is that big?"

"She was in the average range, leaning toward the upper end."

"That's good."

"Stop me if I go too fast," she said.

He was standing so close that she could feel the warmth from his body, smell the scent of his skin. The combination made her senses hum with awareness. Shelby turned the pages and realized she was going too fast but it had nothing to do with looking at pictures.

Luke put his hand on hers to stop her and she felt that touch all the way up her arm. "What?" she asked.

"Go back to the first page," he said. When she did, he pointed to the paper there. "Is that her birth certificate?"

Shelby looked closer. "Not the official one with the raised seal from the county and state. This is the cute one from the hospital with her footprint."

He touched it gently with his finger. "So small."

"Yeah. I'll never forget how scared I was. She wasn't a pet or plant. It was my responsibility to keep her alive." She shook her head. "I couldn't stop thinking that I was just a baby myself. How was I supposed to do that?"

"Yeah. I can see it must have been hard." He turned the page to a picture of Shelby holding Emma in the glider chair where she was no doubt trying to rock her to sleep. "You look tired."

"I've never been so exhausted, before or since. She was up every three hours."

"But your mom helped, right?"

"I was nursing so she couldn't feed Emma." She met his gaze and saw the accusations there. Her mother had many flaws and Shelby knew them better than anyone. But the woman had been there when she'd needed her most and that was something she would defend until hell wouldn't have it. "She was there and supported me in more ways than I can count."

He nodded, then traced a blank line on the birth certificate. "Is there a father's name on the official one?"

No point in lying. "No. But there should be."

"Did your mom support leaving my name off?"

"She had nothing to do with it. In the hospital the nurse asked me if I wanted to name the father and I told her you left and weren't a part of my life." Now the look in his eyes was less angry and more wistful. Sad. "I'll fix it. Your name can be added. I've already looked into how to do that. I have to submit her birth certificate to the Department of Vital Statistics, pay the application and you have to sign an affidavit of paternity."

"So you already researched it."

"Yes."

"Bet your mom isn't happy about that," he said.

She turned and faced him. "What did she say to you when Emma and I were upstairs?"

"That she didn't want me in Emma's life or yours because I would break your hearts."

Shelby put a hand over her mouth. "I can't believe she said that to you. Luke, I'm really sorry. She'll come around."

"I won't hold my breath." He glanced down at the baby picture and there was longing in his eyes.

"I know I said I wasn't going to apologize any

more, but I can't help it. I'm so sorry about everything. I will regret for the rest of my life that you didn't get to hold Emma when she was born." She put her hand on his arm. "Sorry means nothing to you, but it's all I've got. And these pictures. I'll make copies of them for you."

"She still hasn't called me Dad."

"But she said her dad won her a bear," Shelby pointed out. "That's a start. I know it's hard to be patient after missing out on so much, but that's what it will take."

"I was never very patient." His look was a challenge.

"I remember that. I'm hoping you've acquired some in the last ten years."

He lifted one shoulder in a shrug. "Possibly. I'm taking my time with the repairs on this house. Mom didn't do much to it because she was renting it out."

"Oh?" She looked around. "What's on your renovation list?"

"I'm replacing baseboards and trim. Crown molding. None of that is expensive but will make it show better to prospective buyers. According to the real estate agent it will make the place pop."

"Popping is good, I guess." She glanced into the living room. "Looks like painting will happen soon."

"Yeah. I'm going to pick out colors tomorrow." He folded his arms over his chest. "If I asked Emma what would she say is her favorite color?"

"Pink or purple. It's a toss-up." She was going to

throw this out there for the heck of it. In the spirit of helping him know his daughter. "She'd love to go with you and help pick out colors for the wall."

"You think?"

"I'm sure of it."

"Okay," he said. "You can come, too. If you want."

What? He was including her? That made Shelby ridiculously happy. A little giddy. Like a teenager. This couldn't be good and she should say no. But she was so grateful that he didn't seem to hate her, the word just wouldn't come out of her mouth.

"Tomorrow, then," she said.

The next morning Luke poured himself a cup of coffee and looked at the spot where Shelby had stood the night before. She'd been in this house before; used to come over and see his mom. The two of them were friends but his mother didn't know Shelby wasn't supposed to be seeing him. So she was back with baby pictures of Emma, photographs that recorded things he'd missed. Seeing them had stoked the embers of his anger but, oddly enough, it didn't burst into flame. She'd reached out knowing he would probably get ticked off. That was something and he should meet her halfway.

She'd looked so damn sorry about what happened that he was having a hard time not believing she was sincere.

And what the hell had he been thinking to invite her to go along with him and Emma to look at paint?

The answer was that he hadn't been, at least not with his head. He wanted more than anything to give his daughter a father and a sense of family, as much as possible with Shelby. But his plan was the three of them and big gesture stuff—like Disneyland on her birthday, Universal Studios or Legoland. Soccer games. Not the paint store.

But nobody did sweet, soft, warm and sorry like Shelby Richards. And when she was like that he forgot to remember that she knowingly kept his daughter from him.

There was a knock on the glass slider to the outside patio and Emma was standing there. He set his coffee down, then unlocked and opened the door.

"Hey, kid. Why didn't you come to the front door?"

"There's a loose board in the fence. I came that way. It's faster."

Luke knew it well. Then he realized she didn't look her usual in good spirits self. "What's up?"

"I'm goin' to the store with you to look at paint."

"I know."

"Can we go now?" she asked.

"I thought your mom was coming along." There was a part of him anticipating that. He wasn't proud, but it was the truth.

"She might have changed her mind." Emma wouldn't quite look at him.

"Did she tell you she's not coming?"

"Not exactly. But I'm pretty sure she isn't. So we

should just go." Now she turned pleading eyes on him. "Maybe we could get a donut."

Not to blow his own horn, but Luke was a pretty good detective. He'd cracked a lot of cases involving dishonest people who were better liars than this little girl. Something was definitely going on.

"Okay, kid. We need to talk." He picked her up and set her on the island. For just a second, a memory flashed through his mind of his father doing the same thing to him when he was about the same age. So they could talk man-to-man. He shook off the image and folded his arms over his chest. "What's going on?"

"Nothing."

How in the world was it possible for this little girl to look so innocent and guilty as hell at the same time? "I'm not buying that. Why do you want to leave your mom behind?"

"Do I have to tell you?"

"Yes."

She heaved a dramatic sigh and glared at him but his sharp detective skills told him it was directed at her mother. "Mommy won't let me have a donut for breakfast. And she said I have to make my bed and put toys away before we go."

"I see." He nodded, pretending to think it over. But this was classic divide and conquer. He couldn't cancel out her mother's orders even if he didn't agree with them. Which he did, in this case. "Here's the thing, kid. You have to do what your mom says."

"What if it's stupid?"

"She's pretty smart." Although a little nerdy. He remembered what a turn-on that had been. Hell, who was he kidding? She was still a turn-on, one he had every intention of ignoring. "If she tells you to do something, or not do it, I'm sure she has a good reason."

"But why do I have to make my bed? I'm just gonna get in it again later."

"I once heard a commanding officer say that it's the first task in the morning. Your first success. If you can't do little things right, how are you going to do the big things? And if you have a bad day, at least when you come home the bed is made. In the army I had to make my bed every day and I still do it."

"But you're a grown-up."

"Now it's a habit. And I'd have been in big trouble if I didn't. I'm thinking you'll be in big trouble with your mom if you don't."

She looked uncertain now. "I don't like it when she's mad at me."

"Nobody likes it when their mom is mad." He should know. His mom was mad 24-7 after his dad died. Pretty soon she would have another reason. A granddaughter she didn't know about was right here. And he would tell her, after he worked on his own relationship with Emma. When that was more solid he'd deal with his mother.

"Can't you and me just go without her?" she pleaded.

"We could," he agreed. "But would you have any fun knowing you'd be in even more trouble when you got home?"

She thought about that before slowly shaking her head. "I guess not."

"Does she know you're here?"

"No." She looked up then. "I sneaked out when she got in the shower."

He could have gone all day without an image of a naked and wet Shelby stuck in his mind. "Look, if you hurry back, maybe she won't know you left and you can do your chores. No harm, no foul."

"I don't know what that means."

"It's a sports thing. It means if you don't hurt anyone, you don't get a penalty."

"Like a yellow card in soccer?"

"Sort of." He lifted her down, then bent and rested his hands on his knees to meet her gaze. "So, if you do what she asked, maybe we can talk her into getting chicken nuggets and fries for lunch. Not a donut but a consolation prize."

Emma nodded enthusiastically. "See you later."

"I'm looking forward to it."

She started toward the door then turned and threw her arms around his neck. "Bye."

Then she was gone and he had a lump the size of a Toyota in his throat. He felt as if he'd passed a parental test of some kind. A very dad-like sensation came over him.

And the mood stayed with him for a while. When

Shelby and Emma walked over to ride with him, he waited for the hammer to fall but nothing was said about unmade beds and messy rooms. He concluded that his daughter had pulled off her covert mission with a high degree of success. When he lifted her into the rear passenger seat, he winked and she put her hand over her mouth to stifle a giggle.

They had a secret and that made him feel pretty darn good.

When they arrived at the hardware store the three of them went directly to the paint section to look at the choices. Luke knew the brand he wanted so they concentrated their efforts there. Emma skipped down the aisle a short way and was checking out stuff.

In front of him was an almost overwhelming array of colors on cards. Shelby stood beside him and the fragrance of her hair was sweet and floral. When she reached for one of the color cards, her shoulder brushed against his arm. The touch lasted a second but had him wishing for more. He had only himself to blame for it because of that weak moment when he'd said she could come. This was a bad time to want those words back.

Studying the rows of choices she didn't seem to notice the silence. "You didn't ask for my opinion, but I like these shades. They're rich and warm. It just depends on how light or dark you want to go."

He pretended to pore over the card in her hand when it took most of his concentration not to put his arm around her. Ten years ago the movement was automatic and now the more he was around her, the harder he had to work at remembering not to do it.

"Look," he said, "I'm not that fussy. I just want to get the house sold. The Realtor said buyers looking at it need to be able to picture their furniture in it. I took that to mean no black, red or turquoise."

"So you want a shade that goes with everything." She took another card. "These have more yellow. The shades go from cream to gold. This one in the middle is sort of wheat-colored. Kind of serene and peaceful, but still warm earth tones."

"Yeah. I like it." *And the way you smell*, he almost said. But just then Emma came skipping toward them with color cards in her hand.

"Can I pick out the color for my room?"

"Your what now?" Shelby looked at him.

"My room. The one where I'm going to sleep when I spend the night at my dad's." She held them up. "I like these, pink and lavender."

Luke was caught somewhere between horror at the colors she was holding up and euphoria at the progress in her attitude toward him. She'd nearly called him dad. If he gave her a hard negative on this paint thing, would they be back to square one?

"I know what we could do," Emma said excitedly. "Three walls could be pink and one lavender."

Shelby was looking at him and the conflict must have shown because she gave him sympathetic eyes before tackling the problem. "Peanut, your dad is planning to paint every room the same color."

"But why?"

"Because he's fixing it up to sell it. Buyers want to be able to move in and not have to think about re-painting because they don't like the color."

"I think people would like a pink and purple room." Emma got a look he was beginning to recognize as stubborn.

"What if they don't have a little girl? What if there are all boys?" Shelby's voice was patient and reasonable and he had no idea how she did that.

"Boys might like pink."

"Sweetie, the color has to be neutral."

"What does that mean?"

"It means that anything goes with it. Someone might not want to buy the house if they don't like the wall color."

Emma looked at him. "If someone else buys it, that means you won't be staying in the house next door."

"Not there." He glanced at Shelby. "But I'm not leaving town."

"But I like it that you're there," Emma protested.

"You'll still see him all the time," her mom assured her. "We just have to drive. You won't be able to walk over."

"But I like walking over. When I get mad at Mommy I can come over to your house. Like this morning."

Shelby's eyes narrowed on him. "This morning?"

The secret was out. It had been nice while it

lasted. He looked at Emma. "Probably you shouldn't think about a career in the spy sector."

"What happened?" Shelby demanded.

Luke explained why Emma had sneaked over and what he'd discussed with her. Stressing that he had backed Shelby up.

Her expression relaxed and she smiled. "Her bed was made and the toys picked up. And here I thought she was turning into a neat freak. Instead it was you. Nicely done."

"Thank you." Again he got that dad-like feeling and was glad he'd brought her along after all.

He looked at Emma and said, "I'll always be there for you, kid. Whether you can walk over to my house or not. All you have to do is call."

She looked at the color cards in her hand. "Do I need to put these back?"

"Afraid so, sweetie."

He watched Shelby walk her down the aisle to the correct display. His heart melted. That little girl was something else. And he hoped he was becoming important to her, too. Maybe one of these days she would even call him Dad.

Chapter Seven

At dinner that night Shelby was still processing the fact that Emma was so quickly mastering the art of pitting one parent against the other. And the fact that Luke didn't fall for it. He could have thrown her under the bus for a little revenge but he didn't. Probably some instinct told him it wouldn't be good for his daughter. Three cheers for a united front!

The three of them had a really nice time together. After the hardware store where Luke bought his paint—a neutral beige-y color for the walls and white for doors and molding—they were hungry and let Emma pick a place for lunch. Bonding with her father was more important than a single fast-food meal and truthfully Shelby knew better than anyone that forbidding it was the best way to make it more attractive.

While Emma was in the kids' play area, she and Luke had a pleasant conversation. They talked about their jobs, the changes in Huntington Hills over the years and everything in between. Both of them carefully avoided reminiscing about their past relationship. She was glad he didn't bring it up because Emma was bound to notice any emotional shift.

When she and Emma walked in the house close to dinnertime, her mother had been tense and edgy. No doubt the attitude had something to do with her and Emma spending time with Luke. As soon as Emma was comfortable with the situation, Shelby wouldn't be seeing him and her mom could relax.

"Emma, eat your green beans."

"I don't like them, Grammy."

"We all have to do things we don't like."

Shelby figured that remark was directed to her and had something to do with Luke, but she couldn't figure out what. "Your grandmother is right, Emma. You need to eat your vegetables, especially since your lunch today could have been healthier."

"My dad really likes hamburgers, Grammy." Emma speared one bean with her fork and examined it as if the thing was a poisonous insect. "I bet he doesn't eat vegetables."

"I think you're wrong about that. He's pretty strong and wouldn't be if he didn't eat right." His body had changed since he left her. Not that he hadn't been in shape then, but he'd filled out and was more muscular. He was in top physical condition, a fact that didn't go unnoticed. She didn't want to, but she had eyes and hormones. "Your dad has to eat a well-rounded diet and live a healthy lifestyle to look the way he does."

"I want to be healthy like him." The little girl ate her green beans without another word and her grandmother didn't look particularly pleased about it.

"Valentine's Day is coming up." Clearly her mother was changing the topic. "You need to pick out valentine cards for your class, Em."

"I know." She looked thoughtful. "I need to get one for my dad, too."

"Is there going to be a class party this year?" Pam was going for another change in topic. Anything but Luke. "I don't remember seeing a notice from your teacher."

"Yes. Sorry, Grammy. I forgot to give it to Mommy. It's in my backpack." Emma finished the last of her milk and wiped her mouth with her napkin. "Maybe my dad can come to the party. Parents are invited."

"He might have to work," Shelby said.

"But if he's not. You're coming again, right, Grammy?"

"If I can get the time from work." She was the registrar for the junior high school and had never had a problem getting a couple hours off for her granddaughter.

"But you always come," Emma protested.

Shelby had never seen her mom anything but excited about and encouraging of Emma's activities. This was about Luke. And they needed to have a conversation when Emma wasn't around.

The little girl was frowning at her grandmother. "Grammy, why don't you like my dad?"

Oh, boy. She'd noticed the hostile vibe, too. *Don't sugarcoat it, Em*, she thought. Tell her how you really feel. Then again, talking was good. Get the feelings out in the open.

"Oh, Emma, don't be silly." The woman waved her hand dismissively. "Shelby, I heard the high school math and science departments are going to receive grants for more resources."

"It's not a done deal yet, Mom. But we're keeping our fingers crossed."

"Then I will, too—"

"Grammy, I'm not being silly." Emma's little face was all earnest intensity, the way only a nine-year-old could look. "You don't like him."

"I'm not sure why you're saying that, honey." But she looked uncomfortable. "What makes you think I don't like him?"

"Every time I mention him your eyes get weird, like you're mad. And your mouth gets all scrunchy." She met Shelby's gaze across the table. "The way you look at Mommy when you're not happy."

"I hardly ever get mad at your mother." It was true, but yet another deflection. Pam was reaching now, hoping to distract this acutely observant child. "So if you're finished with your dinner—"

"You should tell her, Mom." That got Shelby one of those not-happy looks that her daughter had just described. The woman was clearly annoyed so they might as well air it all out. "You're blowing her off and Emma deserves an answer."

Pam glared at her. "You know very well that it's complicated."

"That's what grown-ups always say to a kid," Emma grumbled.

"Just keep it simple for her," Shelby suggested.

"All right." Her mom thought for a few moments. "A long time ago, before you were born, he made your mother cry."

Emma looked thoughtful. "You mean the way Evan Collins made me cry when he laughed at my freckles?"

"Sort of," her grandmother said. "The thing is, when someone hurts a person you love, it can be worse than if they hurt you."

Score one for Mom making it uncomplicated, Shelby thought. When that little twerp made her daughter cry, she wanted him to pay. It was as easy as an explanation could be. The problem was that Emma had no frame of reference to understand because she wasn't a mom. Shelby had to jump in here.

"Peanut, your dad was a lot younger then and so was I. He said some things that hurt my feelings and Grammy didn't like that. You and I are getting to know him now and he's changed. I cared about him and he left. It made me cry but he had to do what was right for him. Everyone does. And sometimes when that happens people cry. But I got over it."

"Grammy didn't get over it," Emma pointed out.

"She's working on it." Shelby glanced at her mom and the closed-off expression made a lie of that statement.

"I have a great idea, Grammy. You could work on it some more at the valentine party." The eagerness on that little face was pretty hard to resist but her grandmother was doing a good job of it.

"Grammy has to find out if she can get the time off from work," Shelby reminded her. She felt like the diplomat negotiating a peace treaty between two disgruntled nations. "And if you're finished eating, you need to take a bath and get your clothes ready for school. Tomorrow is Monday, remember?"

"But, Mommy, it's too early for my bath."

"Yes, but if you get everything done fast, we'll have time for TV. And popcorn."

"I love popcorn."

"I know." Shelby was pretty sure that the *Parenting for Dummies* handbook didn't recommend bribing a child with food in order to get her out of the room for a sensitive conversation.

Emma slid off her chair and picked up her dishes to clear them from the table. "I'm going to hurry."

"That's my girl."

Shelby waited until she heard the upstairs bathroom door close before speaking. "Mom, what the heck?"

"You're going to have to be more specific, Shelby."

"Okay. Your hostility is showing. This situation is hard enough without that."

"I'm sorry. I can't help it. I love Emma," she said defensively.

"So do I."

"He broke your heart and I can't forgive him for that."

"You can't pretend to be nice?"

"No. So sue me." The woman's eyes blazed with anger.

"That was a long time ago. You never gave him a chance then, but your granddaughter might appreciate you giving him one now."

"I adore that child. With all my heart. I would die before letting anyone hurt her."

"That makes two of us." Shelby blew out a long breath. "And I'm sure this is going to make you nuts, but he is her father and he's doing all the right things."

"A leopard doesn't change its spots."

"Even leopards mature and evolve. Mom, he was a soldier. He's a detective now for the Huntington Hills Police Department. It's hard to get more straight-arrow than that. Doesn't it buy him something?"

"None of that means he's actually different, less selfish than he was then," Pam said stubbornly.

"I think he's earned the right to be given the benefit of the doubt."

"And I disagree."

"If I had told him the truth then, things would be different now." Frustration made her lash out. "And if I'd gotten the letters he wrote to me from basic training, I'm sure I'd have told him I was pregnant." Shelby saw her mother's face go pale. "But you made sure I didn't hear from him, right? You intercepted the letters."

"I did it for you."

"I believe that but it altered the direction of my life. And Emma's. Things would be so different now if he'd been in her life from the beginning." Shelby threw out the first thing that popped into her mind to prove that statement. "His mother never knew she had a granddaughter living right next door. How would you feel if that happened to you?"

Pam's mouth pulled tight for a moment. "I can only think about you and Emma. You're my family."

"Don't you see, Mom? That is about Emma. Luke and his mom are her family, too."

"I can't worry about them."

"Well you should. Sooner or later she's going to find out. There will be consequences. Trust me. If I know about anything, it's that there are always consequences." Shelby stood. "Can you make Emma popcorn, please?"

"Where are you going?"

"A walk. I need to clear my head before saying things I'll be sorry for."

"Shelby, wait—"

She headed for the front door and didn't stop. Hearing her mother admit to keeping Luke's letters from her was a blow. She'd known since that first conversation with Luke and now she knew why she hadn't confronted it before. She owed her mom so much and could never repay her for the love and support.

The idea of resenting the woman who had been there for her through the most difficult time of her life was unthinkable and she didn't want to deal with it. Then Emma had seen the way her grandmother felt about her father and questioned it. At the same time Shelby was grateful to her mother for everything, she was angry that the woman had forced her into a decision with so much collateral damage emotionally.

On the sidewalk she walked quickly past the house next door with Luke's truck in the driveway and all the lights on. She realized that even if he hadn't come back, the question of her father would have to be handled. Emma had already started to ask questions about him. All those years ago she didn't foresee this happening and the choice was made with Emma's best interests at heart. Now she was caught in the middle anyway.

She hated herself for that.

* * *

Luke wouldn't have seen Shelby walk by his house except that he was putting masking tape on the living room window to get ready for painting. He was working twelve-hour shifts at HHPD the next couple days and wanted to get this prep work done and be ready to dive right into this project when he had a couple days off.

Something about Shelby's body language told him this wasn't a leisurely after-dinner stroll. His first reckless instinct was to go after her and find out what was up. Then he checked himself. Their deal was about helping him bond with his daughter and Emma was nowhere in sight, taking away a logical reason to see her. Any intervention from him would have to go under the heading of personal. Smart money said stay out of it. But he'd never been very smart where Shelby was concerned.

"Oh, hell—" He grabbed his jacket tossed over the stairway railing and went outside.

On the porch, he looked in the direction she'd been walking. Down the block he spotted her white T-shirt under a streetlight and jogged after her. Although not running, she was going at a pretty good clip but his strides were longer than hers and he caught up fast.

"Shelby—"

She kept power walking as if she hadn't heard him.

"Shelby, wait up." She seemed to hesitate but finally slowed down and he fell into step beside her. "What's wrong?"

"Nothing."

"You know I'm a cop, right?"

"Yes. But I'm not breaking any laws, so what's your point?" Her voice was clipped and full of irritation.

"I'm pretty good at spotting when someone is lying." Besides, he had known her pretty well and this was what she did if someone upset her. Apparently that hadn't changed. When she didn't respond to his comment, he said, "Clearly something is bothering you."

"Nothing that I can talk to you about."

It was dark except for street and porch lights. The neighborhood was quiet with only an occasional dog barking or car driving by. Luke had no trouble hearing the frustration, anger and hurt in her voice. She'd grown up in the years since they were together and had adult problems, but she sounded the same now as she had then and he found himself reacting the same way. He wanted to fix it.

Just passing under a streetlight, he saw the stubborn tilt of her chin, the tense set to her mouth, and figured he was going to have to put his interrogation skills to work.

"Is Emma okay?"

"I'd have told you if she wasn't."

"Are you having a problem with a student?" God knew he'd been one of those troubled teens who give teachers ulcers and gray hair. But he didn't think that was the case or she'd have shown signs when they were together earlier and then she'd been carefree. Just to cover all the bases he added, "Or a parent?"

"Not a student's parent," she snapped.

"Your parent." He was good at asking questions but she got points for not dodging.

"I had a fight with my mom and we hardly ever do that." She glanced up at him. "You're going to ask what it was about."

"Yeah."

"You."

He'd expected her to suggest he take a flying leap and it surprised him that she didn't. "What about me? Besides the obvious that my being back stirred things up."

"Nothing that didn't need stirring up—" The words stopped because she was shivering.

Luke realized she wasn't wearing a jacket, probably slammed out of the house without one. He moved in front of her and she walked into him.

"What?" she demanded.

"You're cold." He put the jacket he still carried around her shoulders. "And I think we should head back."

"I don't want to go home."

"You don't have to. Let's just head in that direction."

She nodded, turned back the way they'd come and slid her arms into the sleeves that were way too big for her. They walked in silence for a minute or two and she didn't volunteer any more details about what happened to make her so angry.

Back to interrogation 101. "So what got stirred up?"

"You're not going to let this go, are you?"

"No," he said simply.

"Why do you care?" She looked up, studying him.

"Good question." The fact that she was upset shouldn't matter and he didn't want it to. But he couldn't ignore her show of temper either. He chalked it up to being a soldier and cop, in public service. Any other motivation would have been stupid and he wouldn't go deeper.

"I care for two reasons," he said. "Something happened and it was about me. And second, you're the mother of my daughter. Your well-being affects her."

"Fair enough." She nodded absently. "What started it was Emma asking why my mom doesn't like you."

Was it wrong to feel so much satisfaction that Emma was solidly in his corner? "She noticed that, huh?"

"She's very observant." Shelby sighed. "Mom came up with an answer that would be hard for any parent to fault."

"What did she say?"

"That she's mad at you for making me cry."

That punctured his satisfaction balloon. And he couldn't dispute the accusation. The last time he saw Shelby to tell her he joined the army and say goodbye, she'd been crying. He hated that and it had taken every ounce of self-control not to pull her into his arms and tell her he would send for her as soon as he could.

Right now Luke was having similar self-control issues, except this time he was on the other side of her lying to him. "But that's not why you walked out in a huff, is it?"

"No." She stopped and looked up, her big eyes troubled. "She admitted she intercepted your letters because she didn't want me to have contact with you. She knew I'd have second thoughts and tell you I was pregnant."

"I see." He didn't know what else to say.

"She put me in a horrible position where I had very few choices. But I thought I'd reconciled all of that because I know how much she loves me. And she adores Emma."

"But—"

"Hearing her confirm that she interfered and conspired to keep us apart—" She stopped for a moment and looked away. "I just lost it and had to leave."

"I get it."

"That makes one of us. Because part of me—the mom part—understands that she thought she was doing the right thing for her child."

He remembered how angry and bitter he grew as week after week of basic training went by without a letter from Shelby. He'd been lonely. Basic was hard, physically and mentally. He wasn't good with words but the fact that there was absolutely no re-sponse cut deep.

Yeah, he broke it off, but he'd poured out his heart in those letters, trying to fix what he'd done. When he told Shelby about them, she'd been sincerely sur-prised. He knew when someone was lying and she wasn't. The only explanation was that her mother in-tercepted them. There was no positive way to recon-cile what her mother did to him. To them. To Emma.

"I hate to break this to you, Shelby, but there's no way to make what she did right."

"I agree." She folded her arms over her chest. "But think about this. What would we do if Emma was pregnant? I don't know about you, but I want her to go to college."

"Copy that," he said.

"But what if she was going to have a baby and the father was someone we didn't like? Someone we thought would make her miserable. You're a cop and probably see that type all the time."

He did. He responded to all kinds of calls— domestic violence, child neglect, breaking and en-tering. The thought of Emma involved with anyone like that made his chest hurt.

"Shelby," he said, "your mother took choices away from you. From us. That was wrong."

"I'm not saying she was right about you. Just the opposite. You're a good man. But she didn't know that ten years ago." Her look was pleading. "In the same situation, is it possible that we might do what she did? It's a rhetorical question. I don't expect you to answer." She looked up at him, then started walking again. Their houses were in sight now.

Again Luke fell into step beside her. "You were trying to make a point with that question. Let me try to answer it as best I can."

"Good luck."

"It would be easy to say I wouldn't do what she did, but I recognize that my perspective is biased because I'm the one she cut out of Emma's life. She's my daughter and she's a terrific kid. You've done a great job with her and I know your mother has had a big part in raising her." With an effort he tamped down his resentment. "I love Emma. I know I haven't known her very long but she's an easy kid to fall for. I would do anything to protect her. Would I go to the lengths your mother did in order to keep her safe?" He shrugged. "The truth is, I'm not sure how far I would go."

"That's actually very generous of you. I expected something more in the way of 'your mother is a pushy, lying, interfering bitch.'" She smiled and stopped at the end of his driveway.

He grinned. "I would never say that about my daughter's grandmother."

As she stared at his house the humor on her face faded. It had been brief but he still missed the warmth in her eyes. Again the urge to fix what was wrong made him ask, "What's bothering you?"

"You're not the only one who missed out. Just before walking out tonight I asked my mom how she would feel if she had a grandchild she didn't know about."

"What did she say?"

"That she could only think about me and Emma. Her family. I pointed out that your family is Emma's, too." She caught her bottom lip between her teeth for a moment. "I told her that sooner or later your mom was going to know and there would be consequences."

"Yeah."

"Have you told her yet?"

He shook his head. "She's getting settled in Phoenix. And I wanted to get to know Emma better before tackling everything with my mom."

"Okay."

"Just so you know, she'll come here when I break the news."

"I'd expect nothing less."

He put his hand on her arm to stop her when she started to turn away. "One more thing. I'm working the next couple of days. When I'm off, would it be okay for Emma to spend some time with me?"

"Of course," she agreed without hesitation. "I'll let her know. And Luke?"

"Yeah."

"Just so you're forewarned, she wants you to come to the Valentine's Day party at her school. I told her you might be working, so—"

"I'll be there."

"Just like that?" she asked.

"Absolutely."

"Well, thanks for being there for me tonight. It helped to talk."

"I'm glad."

"Good night." She started to walk away, then stopped to take off his jacket and hand it over. "And thanks for this."

"You're welcome."

He watched her walk inside, then crossed the grass and let himself into the house. When he lifted the jacket to toss it back over the stairway railing, he caught a whiff of her fragrance and breathed it in. The scent of Shelby burrowed deep inside him and suddenly he felt a need so strong it nearly brought him to his knees. Feelings he thought long buried weren't quite as squared away as he would like them to be. And he realized something else.

It was getting harder and harder to blame her for the decision she'd made to keep Emma a secret. He was having trouble holding it against her and that was a problem. If he let it go, there would be nothing to keep his feelings for her in check. Then he would be right back where he was ten years ago. Tied up in knots over Shelby.

Chapter Eight

"Hey, Emma, what do you want for dinner?"

Luke had this whole Friday with his daughter. He'd gone to the Valentine's Day party in her classroom earlier and everything had gone off without a hitch. Even though her hostile grandmother attended, too. By mutual, unspoken agreement they'd ignored each other and Emma didn't seem to notice. She'd seemed excited to introduce him as her dad when he helped her pass out her valentines to classmates. Even the sugar buzz overexcitement from a bunch of fourth graders couldn't take the shine off that moment. And when class was dismissed, he got to take her home. That probably put Pam's knickers in a twist which didn't bother him a bit.

Now it was late afternoon and they were shopping for groceries together. This was an occasion because she was going to spend the night at his place for the first time. Her idea and Shelby approved. The house would be sold eventually, but he had bought a twin bed for her. Wherever he ended up after the sale happened, she would still need one.

"What do I want for dinner." Emma was walking beside him next to the rapidly filling shopping basket. She looked up at him. "Can you even cook?"

"I'm hurt you would even ask that question. I've got skills. You can't get takeout every night."

"But you do it a lot." Big dramatic eyes met his own. "I've seen the containers in your refrigerator."

Busted. He could be looking at a future prosecuting attorney. "You're right. I often stop for food before coming home after a shift. It's easier. And I'm usually pretty hungry. Plus, cooking for one is a challenge."

She thought about that and nodded. "But I'm here tonight. That makes two, Dad."

Luke wasn't sure he'd heard right. There were any number of words that rhymed with *dad*—sad, glad, bad, rad. He wanted to ask and make sure she'd just called him that but it would make this a big deal and get weird. The best thing would be to just leave it alone and act cool.

He almost always went to the store with a list but not this time. This day was all about Emma and letting her pick out whatever she wanted. Was he buying her love? Maybe. But he also wanted to know her likes, dislikes and stuff she wouldn't eat even for money.

"Can we get popcorn?" She pointed to a box containing six microwavable bags. "Mommy gets that kind."

"Put it in the basket," he said.

She smiled from ear to ear and proudly took care of it. "Thanks, Dad."

There it was again. As if she'd always been saying it. He was someone's dad. There should be a band playing, a parade, something to mark this momentous occasion. It had to be enough that all of the above was going on inside him. But he still had to feed her tonight. Preferably a well-balanced meal.

"I hate to break this to you, kid, but popcorn isn't dinner. You still haven't told me what you want."

"Because you still haven't told me what you can cook."

"Fair enough." He thought for a moment. "I grill a lot. Steak, ribs, hamburgers and hot dogs."

"Do you burn them?" She wrinkled her nose in disapproval.

"Not usually."

"Mommy likes them that way but I think they're gross."

Luke remembered that. Shelby had managed to sneak out for a Fourth of July picnic at the park. She asked for the most well-done hot dog and he'd teased her about eating charred tubes. She was unaffected by his mocking and savored it while he enjoyed watching her, wanting more than anything to be alone with her. And kiss her until they both lost control. Then his daughter's voice punctured that sensuous spell.

"What about spaghetti?" Emma pointed to the pasta on the shelf.

"That depends. How do you like sauce in a jar?"

"Grammy uses that and it's good." The little girl shrugged.

As much as he didn't want to hear anything about what that woman did, he couldn't afford to ignore the tips. "Should I get some?"

"No." She kept walking beside him, her hand on the basket.

"It's getting pretty close to decision time. We're almost out of the store."

"What do you feel like?" she asked.

He felt like he'd missed out on an awful lot. The years when she'd formed her opinions he hadn't been around.

The opportunity to have a positive influence had been missed then, but he intended to make up for that now.

"Dad?"

Hearing her call him that would never get old. But the question in her voice made Luke glance down. "What?"

"You have a funny look on your face and you didn't answer my question."

"Sorry. I was thinking about something else and the question was what I want for dinner." He said the first thing that popped into his mind. "Hamburgers and hot dogs."

"That's what I was going to say." Her eyes were wide and wondering.

"It must be a sign." He grinned down at her and brushed a knuckle across her freckled cheek. "We'll circle back to the bread aisle and get rolls after we pick up the burgers. Do you like the works on your hot dog?"

"What's that?"

"Mustard, relish, onions, sauerkraut and chili."

"No. Mustard."

"Okay we need to get some, then. The refrigerator is pretty empty."

"I know." Emma was well on her way to a PhD in sarcasm. "Only takeout boxes."

"Right. Don't judge."

They picked up dinner stuff along with fruit and were now eyeing the vegetables. Her eyes said she would rather be in any other aisle.

He stopped the basket. "How about Brussels sprouts?"

"No."

"Have you ever tried them?" he asked.

"Once. Sort of. Grammy made me. There was one leaf stuck to my pork chop and it was really gross."

"So you didn't try a whole one?"

She shook her head. "I thought I was going to throw up."

"So that's a hard negative on Brussels sprouts. Understood." That one went into the "couldn't pay her enough to eat them" file. "Good. I don't know how to cook them."

Her eyes narrowed. "Were you teasing me?"

"Maybe." He grinned. "You're a smart kid."

That put a smile on her face and a skip in her step. The combination made him putty in her hands for the negotiations about chips, ice cream and powdered-sugar donuts for breakfast. After she'd called him dad he would have bought her the moon, but he had a feeling telling her that would be a mistake. After paying for the groceries they headed home and Emma insisted on helping carry everything inside. He had to shift items in the bags to make sure they weren't too heavy for her. It took longer than if he'd done the hauling himself but he wouldn't trade the father/daughter teamwork experience for anything.

Once the bags were in the kitchen she couldn't be talked out of helping to unpack and put things away. She chattered about school, soccer and her friends. Which was when everything took a turn.

Emma pulled the package of hot dogs out of a bag. "Karen loves these."

"Isn't she the goalkeeper on your team?"

"Yes. And she's my BFF."

"BFF? That's a test, right?" he asked. "You think I don't know that means best friends forever?"

"Maybe." Emma grinned mischievously. "Can she sleep over tonight?"

Whoa, slow down. Several things ran through Luke's mind one after the other. This was a more complicated decision than the dinner menu. He wanted to say no—this is my time with you and I'm not sharing. Call me selfish. And finally, WWSD—what would Shelby do?

Luke thought about the time he'd spent with her and Emma, watching her deal with their daughter. More than once Emma had asked for something out of the blue and her mother automatically said, "Let me think about it." The words seemed magical. As far as he knew that response stopped everything right there. "Is it okay?" Emma asked again.

Those pleading eyes were the biggest challenge he'd ever faced but he had this. "Let me think about it."

"But Dad—" Just like that Emma's pleading look turned fiercely defiant. "I want her to."

Wait, that wasn't supposed to happen. Let's try this again. "I said I need to think about it."

"But she hasn't slept over in a long time. And we can have hot dogs and popcorn."

"I did buy all that stuff—"

"So, I'll call her and see if she can come over." The little girl moved toward the phone on the counter.

"Wait, Emma, I didn't say yes."

"You didn't say no," she pointed out.

But he wanted to. Why couldn't he? Stupid question. He wanted her to like him. But this didn't feel right. "I was looking forward to having dinner just the two of us."

"Then it would be three of us. You'll like her," she promised.

"Her parents don't know me. And maybe they wouldn't want her to go to a stranger's house. Especially on such short notice." He was dancing around a negative and hoping she would just let this go.

"They won't care." She called his bluff. "Please, Dad."

He really didn't like this idea. "How about if we plan it another time?"

"But I want her to come over tonight."

He knew when he was boxed in. As much as he didn't want to, he had to say it. "No, Emma, not this time."

"You're mean and I'm not staying here with you." Angry tears welled in her eyes before she stomped out of the kitchen toward the front door. "I hate you and I wish you weren't my dad."

And then she was gone. One minute he'd been on top of the world, the next he was flattened by a freckle-faced nine-year-old. He felt as if he had the wind knocked out of him and his head was spinning.

When he pulled it together, he realized he needed to call Shelby and took out his cell phone. He hit speed dial and got her voicemail. This wasn't good and he had to explain what happened. Pacing the room he weighed his options and figured going over and speaking face-to-face was the best. But before he could do that there was a knock. He opened the door and Shelby was there with Emma.

"Hi. She told me you were mean and she doesn't want to stay here."

"Let me explain—"

She held up a hand to stop him. "I know what happened. And she has something to say to you. Emma?"

The little girl wouldn't look at him. "I'm sorry I said I hate you."

"And?" Shelby prompted.

"I shouldn't have asked for a sleepover without giving you more warning."

"Good." Her mother gave the small shoulders a reassuring squeeze. "Now go wash your face and hands for dinner."

"Okay." She gave him a hostile look then moved past him and went upstairs.

He heard the bathroom door close, then met Shelby's gaze. "You're letting her stay here tonight?"

"Of course. That's what we agreed to do and she was the one who suggested it." She smiled sympathetically. "The honeymoon is over. For what it's worth, you did the right thing."

"She called me dad for the first time today."

"Oh, Luke—" Shelby put her hand on his arm. "I'm so glad."

"I thought I was home free. First the valentine

party at school when she introduced me as her dad. Then she just said it as if calling me dad was the most natural thing in the world. Then—boom."

"Don't you see? She was testing you. By telling her no you actually earned your dad stripes."

"But she hates me."

"No, she doesn't." Her expression was surprisingly tender. "She's just mad. For what it's worth she's tired, too. That will pass because she didn't really mean it."

"I'll have to take your word on that." He didn't mean to sound bitter but it came out that way.

"It's up to us to teach her right from wrong. You're a cop. Your job is all about people who didn't learn that lesson. We have to give her parameters. That's *our* job. Welcome to the wonderful world of parenthood."

"Thanks, I think." He put his hand over hers, where she'd left it on his arm. "Thanks for bringing her back. And the pep talk."

"You're welcome." She smiled. "And just pretend nothing happened. She'll shake it off."

"Okay."

Shelby said good-night and left. For the second time Luke's head was spinning. This night hadn't gone perfectly, far from it. But things could have been worse if Emma's mother had handled it differently. He was a cop and wanted things to be black-and-white, right or wrong. Nothing about this fit into either category. It was all gray area, including an attraction to Shelby that just wouldn't leave him alone.

Later that night Shelby texted Luke to see if it was too late to talk and within seconds her cell vibrated and his caller ID popped up on her phone. She answered right away.

"Hi," she said. "How's it going over there? Is the cold war still—cold?"

He laughed. "She got over it. Just like you said she would. She's sound asleep."

His deep voice sent shivers down her spine and her chest suddenly felt tight. Just an involuntary reaction that she would control if she could. But somehow she managed to blow it every time.

"I'm so glad everything settled down," she finally said.

"Are you calling to initiate a welfare check on a dad in training or is there another reason?"

"I forgot something." When there was silence on the other end of the line, she went on. "I told you about her friend's birthday party tomorrow."

"Yeah. I have the address where to drop her off."

"I didn't put the gift in her backpack with her clothes."

"She can run over in the morning to get it," he said.

"I won't be home. I'm tutoring a student who is currently failing my class. And Mom will be gone, too. I thought it best to make sure this is handled tonight."

"Sure."

"Would it be okay if I bring it over now?"

"That's fine." Did he sound annoyed? It was hard to tell.

"Are you sure? I know it's a little late. I can just leave it on the porch—"

"Shelby, it's really all right. I'm a night owl. Staying up late is SOP for me."

"It's what now?"

"Standard operating procedure. I'll be up for a while. Come on over. I'll pour you a glass of wine."

"Oh, I don't know about—" She suddenly realized he hung up and she was talking to dead air.

Shelby didn't know what to make of this "I'll pour you a glass of wine" Luke versus the angry and resentful man who swore he would never forgive her. Part of her wanted to ding dong ditch him—put the birthday gift on his porch, ring the bell and run. The other part wanted to spend time with a handsome man who fascinated her and also happened to be the father of her child.

Since she had to be a grown-up and face him, she'd best get herself together and see whether or not the wine-pouring, smooth-talking guy she'd just talked to was an alien imposter impersonating the real Luke.

Shelby grabbed the brightly wrapped package then headed to his house, her heart beating faster than a hummingbird's wings. Standing outside the door she took a big breath before knocking softly. He answered almost immediately.

"Hi." He smiled and it was friendly in a way he hadn't been when Emma wasn't present.

Shelby held out the present. "And, just so you know, she packed her favorite outfit to wear to the party so don't let her try and pull a fast one tomorrow because she changed her mind. Call if there are any—"

"Shelby, take a breath. I think I can roll with this." He angled his head toward the interior of the house. "Do you want to come in?"

"It's late. I really shouldn't—"

"Why?" His dark eyes challenged.

"Do I need a reason? Isn't it enough that I'm giving you an out? A chance to think better of this."

"I have thought better. It would be nice to have some company." He glanced over at her house and one corner of his mouth curved up. "Did you sneak out?"

She laughed. "Mom is asleep, so I'm not sure that meets the definition of sneaking."

He stepped back to let her pass and glanced at the living room with plastic drop cloths, paint cans, rollers, pans and other supplies for the job. "There's no place to sit in here. Let's go in the kitchen. I've got bar stools for the island."

He set the party gift on the bottom stair then headed to the back of the house. She followed and wondered whether or not it was wrong to go fangirl admiring his butt and broad shoulders. Right, wrong, indifferent didn't matter because the feeling wasn't a conscious choice. It just happened and she blamed her hormones.

As promised there was a glass of wine, a tumbler actually, already sitting on the island. He looked at it and shrugged. "I don't have fancy glasses. Hope you like red."

"I do." She sat on one of the bar stools and noticed a greeting card standing up on the island. "I see she gave you your valentine card."

He smiled. "Yeah. That's a first."

"It took her a long time to pick it out." She took the tumbler of wine he handed over.

"I'll put it in the scrapbook."

"I never thought of you as a scrapbook kind of guy," Shelby said.

"I've never been a father before." Luke opened the refrigerator and grabbed a longneck bottle of beer, then twisted off the cap before sitting beside her.

She took a sip of wine because after that she didn't know what to say. Thoughts rolled through her mind but there was only one thing she wanted to know. With their troubled history and his hard feelings about the past it didn't seem possible that she could make the situation worse by asking straight-out.

So she did. "Why are you not glaring at me any-more? What's with the glass of wine? You're being nice and that makes me nervous."

"Glaring, huh?"

"Yes. It could be your superpower. You're very good at it."

"For the record I stopped glaring a while ago." He sipped from his beer. "And the wine is just my way of saying thank-you."

"For what?"

"The valentine card. Making sure she could pick one out for me today. And earlier. You could have taken advantage of Emma's meltdown and used it against me. Encouraged her not to come back."

"Why would I do that?" she asked.

He shrugged. "To keep her from me."

"You're her father. And in case you haven't noticed, she's pretty stubborn and headstrong. She's not going to be kept away if she doesn't want to be," Shelby assured him.

"Still, you did just the opposite."

"Besides the fact that it was the right thing to do, we have a deal. I agreed to help you bond with Emma." She toyed with the tumbler in front of her. "I'm holding up my end of the bargain."

"The truth is that the chip on my shoulder got real heavy when Emma said she hated me and stomped back over to your house. I was really feeling the victim and wallowing in being left out of her life for the last nine years. Then you brought her back, got her to grudgingly apologize and said what you said about being her parent. I realized it wasn't just the good stuff I'd missed. There had to have been bad, too, and you handled that by yourself."

She thought about it and nodded. "You missed the health scare when she was just a few months old and had her first cold and fever. That was scary. But even worse was the stomach bug she caught that put her in the hospital. That's when I found out that nineteen-month-olds dehydrate fast and you can't take any chances when they can't keep liquids down."

"I can't even imagine how you felt."

She would never forget it. "You also weren't here for the bumps, bruises, mean kids. It was all really hard."

"It has to be said that you've done a great job with her, Shel. And I saw you in action when you brought her back tonight."

"Thanks. And I say again that you also did pretty awesome earlier." She held up her glass. "Let's drink to co-parenting and having each other's backs."

He touched his bottle to her glass, then drank. She was fascinated by the way the muscles in his strong neck moved when he swallowed. Their shoulders brushed and sparks flew. She prayed it was nothing more than static electricity. Things were complicated enough without it being more.

"Speaking of having your back—" He set his beer bottle down on the island and met her gaze. "I told my mother about Emma. That she's mine."

"Oh." She thought about the ramifications of that.

"So you're warning me that she hired a hit man to take me out?"

"How did you know?" Then he grinned. "Just kidding."

"Not funny." But she probably deserved that and more. "How did she take it?"

"Truthfully, she didn't say much over the phone. I think she's saving everything for the in-person tongue-lashing." He met her gaze. "She's driving in from Phoenix next week."

"I see."

"She wants to meet Emma," he said.

"Of course. I'll make sure she's available."

He reached over and put his hand on hers. "I'll be there, Shelby. I meant what I said about having your back."

He'd left her once. It wasn't fair to compare this to what happened when he joined the army, when he didn't know she was pregnant. But the result was the same. She'd handled everything then and expected she would do the same now.

"It's okay, Luke. I can handle things by myself. I learned how when you said you didn't want to see me anymore."

"About that, Shelby—" He turned the beer bottle with his fingers. "I'd like to set the record straight once and for all. I pulled the plug on us to protect you from me. And I was leaving. Your mom was right. I was on the edge and could have gone either way. I didn't want you to go down with me. I cared a lot about you."

She was stunned. "I wish you'd told me. We could have faced it together."

"I'm a loner."

"You may have been that way once, but not now." Shelby couldn't read his eyes and didn't know if they reflected regret or resistance. "If only I'd known—"

"What?"

"If I'd known how you felt, nothing could have prevented me from telling you I was pregnant." She saw his eyes narrow, and added, "I'm not saying it's your fault. But it would have made a difference."

"Would it?" Luke kept turning the bottle in front of him on the island.

"I don't know about you, but when we were together then, the drama, the feelings, the angst were so big. It was consuming. Everything else was pushed out and there was only room for you and me."

"Yeah, I remember. But—" He looked sideways and met her gaze. "Now we're mature adults. Rational and reasonable."

"I know, right?" She smiled but wasn't feeling it.

She was shaken by the fact that he'd left to save her from himself. A selfless and heroic impulse. But this revelation opened the floodgates of long-suppressed emotions. Feelings she never expected to have again. She remembered wanting him more than her next breath, as if he was the power source that made her heart beat.

He was opening up now like he never had before and the might-have-beens weighed on her heart. All those years ago if she'd been honest with him and he'd explained that he cared enough to walk away, they might have had a chance. But not now.

Shelby made a mistake and he would never forgive her. Without trust, all the chemistry bubbling between them would just blow up in her face. It was a darn good thing that she was a mature woman now and he couldn't crush her heart twice.

Chapter Nine

Shelby had never been quite this nervous. Oh, there had been anxious times like anticipating childbirth or sending Emma to preschool and kindergarten. But sitting in a booth waiting for Luke to show up with his mother took top spot in the history of apprehensive moments.

She and Luke had strategized the location for this first meeting between Emma and his mom, her other grandmother, and decided neutral territory would be best. This was a kid-friendly pizza place with games, a jumping house and the bacteria capital of the world ball pit. If things got heated and intense, there would be a distraction for Emma and Shelby would worry about the black plague when and if it happened. They'd agreed on a time when both of them would be finished with work and now here she was with their daughter.

"Mommy, when are they gonna get here?"

"Are you hungry?"

"A little. But I want to go play and you said I can't until after I meet her."

"Her" being the paternal grandmother. "I'm sure your dad will be here any minute."

"What's she like?" Emma was sitting on the bench seat beside her.

"I told you, peanut, she's a very nice lady."

Luke hadn't gotten along with the woman, but Shelby had spent a little time with her. Donna McCoy was always pleasant to her and teased her son about why he couldn't be an A student like she was. Then her mom found out they were seeing each other and she'd been forbidden to have anything to do with him or his family. Pam had pretended there was an empty lot where the McCoy house stood.

Shelby had no idea what to expect now and was prepared to get her daughter out of there at the first sign of hostility. But she couldn't tell Emma that.

"I'm sure she's going to love you." Shelby put aside her misgivings and infused her tone with as much reassurance as possible. "How could she not? You're fantastic."

"You have to say that. You're my mom."

"I don't have to say anything. But I'm the first one to tell you when your attitude needs adjustment. If

I don't hesitate to tell you the bad stuff, you can believe me about the good things. Right?"

"But she doesn't know me."

Apparently Shelby wasn't the only one who was nervous. She and Luke didn't hide anything from Emma. They'd given her the facts: he went into the army and didn't know Shelby was going to have a baby. He agreed with her that their daughter only needed basic details because she was too young to really understand the emotions. If Emma had questions they tried to answer honestly.

"She knows you're her granddaughter," Shelby said. "You know how much Grammy loves you. Your dad's mother will, too. Grandparents love to spoil their grandchildren."

"Maybe she'll buy me a scooter." This was the first spark of excitement since they'd left home.

"Don't you dare ask her for anything. Especially not the first time you meet her."

Emma grinned. "I was teasing you, Mom."

"Very funny." Shelby tried not to smile but couldn't help herself.

"But it could happen. Dad bought me stuff," the little girl pointed out.

"He did and I talked to him about that. It's emotionally complicated. What you need to know is that you are not allowed to hold your affections hostage from your grandmother in return for a scooter."

"I'm not sure what that means."

"Like I said, you're a little young to understand.

Just don't mention that you want a scooter and everything will be fine."

"I can do that," Emma agreed.

"I thought so."

She hugged the little girl close for a moment, then noticed Luke coming toward them. His mother looked a little older and her brown hair was cut short. There was no mistaking the frown on her face and the way it made her dark eyes glitter with disapproval. Shelby was about to get what was coming to her and this had been nine years in the making.

The two of them stopped at the end of the booth and Shelby's heart started to hammer. She wondered if she should stand but it wasn't as if the woman was going to hug her. As the three adults stared awkwardly at each other, Emma broke the silence first.

"Hi, Dad. Is this my other grandmother?"

"Yes. My mother, Donna." He looked at the woman. "Mom, you remember Shelby and this is our daughter, Emma."

"Emma—" Her voice caught as she looked at the little girl. "You're beautiful. I'm very happy to meet you."

"Please sit down, Mrs. McCoy," Shelby said. "We've been waiting until you arrived to order."

"I'm hungry," Emma told them.

The older woman slid into the booth across from Emma and Luke sat beside her on the bench seat. His expression was hard to read. Shelby would like to know what he and his mom had said, then figured it didn't matter. The woman couldn't have been happy. No doubt she was looking for a target to vent her displeasure on and she was very grateful for Luke's presence.

"What kind of pizza do you like, Emma?" Donna was staring at her granddaughter with very much the same expression her son had the first time he'd seen Emma. Looking for a family resemblance and seeing it immediately. "Your father used to like sausage and black olives."

"That's my favorite, too," the little girl said. "Mommy, can I have a soda?"

Shelby didn't usually let her and knew Emma was taking advantage of the situation. But it's not like she asked for a scooter. "Just this once. Because it's a special occasion. But let's get a lemon-lime, something without caffeine, okay?"

"Thank you, Mommy."

Donna nodded slightly and there was grudging approval in her eyes. She smiled at her granddaughter. "Your father had trouble going to sleep if he had too much sugar at bedtime. Sometimes he would try to sneak it."

"Did you catch him?" Emma wanted to know.

"Not every time," she admitted. "But I always knew."

"My mom always knows, too," Emma said. "I don't know how."

"It's a secret," Donna told her.

Shelby noticed then that the woman wouldn't even

look at her. She glanced at Luke and saw sympathy in his eyes.

"Let's get that pizza ordered." He signaled for one of the servers and gave her a list of what drinks and food they wanted. Then they were alone again, with another awkward silence that was setting a pattern.

"So, Mrs. McCoy," Shelby said, "how do you like your new home in Phoenix?"

The woman smiled at Emma but when she shifted her gaze to Shelby her expression hardened. "It's a very nice adult community. The weather so far is wonderful, but I know it's going to get hot. The house is smaller, easier to maintain but the distance between there and Huntington Hills seems very far now."

Meaning not right next door where she would have been closer to this child. And her sharp gaze said she was acutely aware that she could have known her granddaughter and established a bond but had been deliberately deprived.

"At least you can drive here for visits, Mom. And Emma and I can come to see you at your place. Right?"

He was looking at Shelby for a response but Emma said, "Cool!"

If this had come up before Luke admitted he didn't just miss the highs of parenting but had also escaped the lows, Shelby might have resisted the idea. It had hit her more intensely how much precious time Luke and his mom had lost. How every experience, good and bad, makes a relationship. Agreeing to visits with her grandmother was the least Shelby could do.

"I think that's a wonderful idea," she said. "Emma has never been to Arizona. You could show her the Grand Canyon."

"Can we, Dad?" Emma looked excited.

"I don't see why not. That's a great idea, Shelby. What do you think, Mom?"

"Wish I'd thought of it." The words were sort of a compliment but her expression said she'd rather eat cardboard than admit to that.

They made small talk about things to see in Phoenix until the food arrived. All of them took slices of pizza but only Emma ate. She wolfed hers down and then asked to go play the games. Luke gave her money and she knew how to buy tokens to put in the machines. Thank goodness she seemed oblivious to the adult undercurrents. As soon as she was out of earshot the real conversation started.

Donna lasered her with a judgmental look. "I have to be honest—"

"Of course." Shelby knew she owed this woman the chance to vent without interruption.

"I don't know how it's possible to be so angry and so thankful at the same time."

Half of that statement was a shocking surprise and considering the stunned expression on Luke's face he felt the same way. "Thankful, Mom?"

"Yes. Emma is absolutely adorable." Donna

glanced sideways. "I'd given up on you giving me any grandchildren because I suspected it was something you knew I wanted so badly. And she's completely wonderful. At the same time I'm furious that she was growing up here in Huntington Hills, in the house next door to where you grew up and I never knew. That's not on you, son." She glared at Shelby. "How could you do such a thing?"

Shelby thought she'd been prepared for this, for his mother to take her best shot. But she recognized how very wrong she was when tears burned her eyes. "I'm sorry—"

Something flashed across Luke's face when he glanced at his mother. "Mom, I told you what happened. She was young and felt there was nowhere to turn."

Donna gave him an exasperated look. "You're not upset?"

"Of course. At least I was." Past tense was noteworthy. "But I've come to terms with the fact that there's nothing to be done except move on."

"That's easy for you to say."

"Actually it's not, Mom. It took a while, but the first time Emma called me dad—" He shook his head. "I can't describe the feeling."

"I can't describe my emotions either," she said angrily. "I'm alternately indignant and ecstatic. She's so sweet and smart and beautiful."

"Shelby is a great mom," he said.

And she almost cried again, this time from gratitude that Luke had her back. The McCoys could have piled on the insults and outrage and she would have deserved every bit of it. But he was not only protective, he was complimentary.

Emma came running back then and the conversation stopped. "Can I go in the ball pit?"

Shelby and Donna said together, "It's full of germs."

The little girl sighed and gave her father a look that said "Help me out here."

"It's probably time we head home," he said instead. "You have school tomorrow."

"Okay." She looked disappointed for a moment then said to Donna, "Will you be here tomorrow?"

"Yes. I'm staying for a few days."

"Then I can come over and visit after school tomorrow?"

"Of course you can. I would love that," Donna said.

"That's a great idea, peanut." Shelby made sure the woman knew she wouldn't stand in the way of her seeing her grandchild.

Luke took care of the bill and they all filed out of the restaurant to the parking lot. Emma insisted on riding with her dad and Donna. Even if Shelby wanted to say no, she couldn't. Besides, in ten minutes they'd be home. Neighbors.

Shelby realized that was a double-edged sword when they pulled into their respective driveways side by side. Her mother came out of the house, a sign

Pam had been watching for them. She'd been less than thrilled about being left out tonight and clearly intended to change that now.

"How did it go?" She walked closer as Shelby exited the car and glanced into the empty back seat. "Where's Emma?"

"Here I am, Grammy." She had Donna's hand and was pulling the other woman over to them. "This is my other grandmother."

"Hi, Pam." She looked down at Emma. "We met a long time ago."

Her mother looked stern and steely, but her voice was neutral when she said, "Hello, Donna."

Emma looked up at her "new" grandmother. "I don't know what to call you."

"Grammy is taken," Pam said.

Donna's eyes narrowed. "That's the one I wanted."

"I could call you Grandma," the little girl suggested. "Or Gran."

"I love Gran." She smiled down at her granddaughter.

"Me, too." Emma hugged her. "Good night. See you tomorrow, Gran."

"I can't wait." Donna looked at the woman who'd once been her neighbor. "I hope you don't have a problem with me spending time with her."

"No." Pam started to say more but looked at Shelby and sighed. "Of course you should get to know her."

Shelby was surprised that her mother had backed

down. The woman was so stubborn she'd expected resistance. Maybe it was a sign that she shouldn't sell hope short.

After watching Emma and Shelby go inside, Luke and his mom went home. They hadn't had much chance to talk since she'd arrived from Phoenix not too long before the arranged meeting time with Shelby and Emma. He was dreading the conversation he was about to have with her, but there was no way to avoid it.

He put his mother's suitcase in Emma's room then walked into the kitchen where he found Donna staring out the window into the backyard. After all these years it was weird being under the same roof again, where they'd butted heads so often. She would never admit it but he knew she blamed him for his father's death.

"I put your things upstairs."

She jumped and turned around. "You startled me. I'm not used to hearing your voice here. Everything feels different. Empty. It's been a long time since we lived in this house."

"I was just thinking the same thing." And he didn't want to talk about it because a fight was the last thing he wanted. All he had to do was get through a couple of days and she would leave. "Can I get you something? Water, soda, wine?"

"Since when do you have wine? I thought you were a beer guy."

He didn't want to admit the real reason he had it. "I keep some for guests."

"You consider Shelby a guest?" She walked over to the island and there was a gleam in her eyes. "It's for her, right?"

"What does it matter?"

"Because I saw the way you looked at her." She sat on one of the bar stools.

"It would have been rude not to look at her during dinner tonight. The way you did." He'd noticed and knew Shelby did, too. Damned if he didn't feel sorry for her. What was up with that?

"Luke, she kept Emma a secret from us. Am I not allowed to have a reaction to that?"

"And wine it is," he said. "I don't have any fancy glasses."

"I don't care."

He opened the bottle and poured a lot into a tumbler, then set it in front of her. "Of course you're allowed to have feelings, Mom. I understand you're still processing."

"It took you quite a while to tell me about all this. Why?"

"I wanted to get to know Emma and deal with being her father before sharing the news."

She took a sip of wine, then held the glass between her hands. "I can understand that."

"Really?" In his experience, understanding wasn't the way she rolled.

"Don't sound so surprised. You found out you're

a father to a nine-year-old girl and wanted to feel in control of the situation."

He was standing across from her with the island between them. Who was this woman and what had she done with his mother? "How did you know that?"

"It's what you do, what you've always done since you were a little boy." She smiled. "I can tell by the look on your face that I surprised you again."

"Yes."

"I'm your mother. It's my job to know you better than anyone."

"I've changed since the army. We haven't spent enough time together for you to know me much better than you did before."

She looked thoughtful for a few moments. "You're more mature, disciplined and conscientious. But you're the same sensitive boy trying to pretend nothing bothers you. You're a lot like your dad."

"I don't want to talk about him—"

"Tough." She gave him a look, daring him to push back. "It's way past time we talked about what happened."

Here we go, he thought. The part he had not been looking forward to. He'd make it quick. "He died in a car accident."

"I know that, but—"

"But nothing." She was right. This part needed to be said. It had been burning a hole in his gut since the day he'd lost his father. "I was arguing with dad. I don't even remember what I wanted but he said no. I wouldn't accept that and he was distracted. If he hadn't been, he would have avoided the car that ran the stop sign. The truth is it was my fault and you blame me. You never forgave me for surviving when he didn't."

"Oh, Luke—" She couldn't have looked more shocked if he'd slapped her. "You're wrong. So very wrong."

"You changed after dad was killed."

"Of course. I lost the love of my life, my husband and best friend. The other driver was proven to be at fault. I never blamed you. My heart was broken but full of gratitude at the same time because I still had you."

"You treated me differently." The emotions suddenly stirred up inside him made his words an indictment. "All we did was fight."

"I treated you differently because I'm your mother and I had to. You started acting differently. Rebelling. Taking chances. Your grades suffered and you gravitated to a group of kids who made it their mission in life to break the rules. It would have killed me to lose you, too." She sighed. "I was the only one standing between you and disaster."

"Murph was there."

"Because I reached out to him, asked him to keep an eye on you," she said.

"He was the one who floated the plan to join the army."

She nodded. "It was my idea."

"Because you wanted me gone," he accused.

"No." She took a shuddering breath and tears filled her eyes. "I wanted you to have structure, stability, discipline that you wouldn't accept from me. You were all I had left of your father. If letting you go was the only way to keep you safe, then so be it."

He stared at her as the truth sank in. "Enlisting was your suggestion?"

She nodded. "But you wouldn't have listened to me so I asked Murph to bring it up."

"I thought you hated me, that I was a reminder of dad. So, you didn't want me out of the house?"

"No," she said simply. "I love you, Luke."

He had never once thought about what his belligerent attitude and bad behavior was doing to his mother. Maybe now that he had a child it was sinking in. Or he'd simply grown up enough to stop being an ass. He moved around the island and leaned over to hug her. "I'm sorry, Mom. For everything. I love you, too."

She held on for several moments, then gave his shoulder a quick pat before letting him go. After brushing the tears from her cheeks, she said, "Now you're a father."

"Yeah." He rubbed a hand over the back of his neck. "I've never missed dad more. I sure would like to talk to him now."

"He's still here. I see it in how you interact with Emma. And she's terrific, by the way." Then the tender look faded and her mouth twisted with disapproval. "Shelby should have told you she was pregnant. It's wrong that she didn't."

"Mom, she had her reasons. And her mother put pressure on her." He explained what Shelby had faced at seventeen, being pregnant and threatened with the loss of her only support system. "Try and put yourself in her shoes."

"I'm sure she must have been scared." Donna's expression clearly showed she was reluctant to admit that.

"Yeah. She said the last time we saw each other when I told her I joined the army, she was planning to tell me about the baby, against her mother's wishes."

"But you made your announcement first," she guessed. "Do you believe her?"

"Yes." There were questions in her eyes so he attempted to put his gut feeling into words. "Since the truth came out, she's done everything possible to help me bond with Emma. She hasn't refused any request I've made and lets me see her whenever I want. I'm a detective, Mom. It's my job to know when someone is lying. When she says she regrets the decision, I have no doubt she's telling the truth."

"Okay." She nodded. "I'm incredibly proud of you and I trust your judgment. I just wish—"

"What?"

"I've lost so much time with my granddaughter. I never got to hold her when she was a baby—" Her voice broke and she looked away for a moment. Then she met his gaze. "She looks like you."

"That seems to be the consensus."

"Shelby used to come over and talk to me from time to time." She took a sip of wine. "Then she didn't. I knew the two of you were seeing each other and it went badly—"

"How did you know that?"

"Oh, please." She smiled. "I was doing covert surveillance before you knew it was a thing. You were over the moon happy, then you looked as if you'd lost your best and only friend."

That pretty much described how he felt when he told her they were over. "I broke it off. For her. Her mother didn't approve of me and she was right. At the time. Even I knew Shelby deserved someone better."

"And apparently she tried to find that someone. After you left I happened to see her get picked up by a boy a few times. In my mind she'd moved on. Then I decided to buy a condo and rent out the house. I never saw Shelby again until tonight. I saw Emma once. If only I'd known—"

"Don't, Mom. You'll make yourself crazy."

"I guess you're right about me still processing."

He got a beer from the refrigerator, twisted off the cap, then sat down on the stool beside her. "Now that you know about Emma, are you sure about listing the house? I haven't yet since I'm still fixing it up. For what it's worth, I think you should. There's a lot of bad memories here."

"Good ones, too. Think about it. Your dad."

Countless emotions crossed her face—joy, sorrow, humor.

He remembered his dad playing catch with him after work. A new bike under the Christmas tree in front of the living room window. Squeezing through that loose board in the backyard fence that his mom had nagged about but his father never got around to fixing. He'd taken advantage of it to sneak over and see Shelby. And this house would always be a painful reminder of his decision to let her go.

"Yeah, I guess," he said.

"I'll leave the decision up to you." She shrugged. "And for the record, you should have told me you blamed yourself for the accident. I couldn't reassure you when I didn't know how you felt. We should have talked about this and cleared the air a long time ago."

"You're right." He held up his beer and she touched her glass to it in a silent toast of agreement.

"Just remember, whether or not you sell, those memories are a part of you. Leaving this house won't erase the past. If finding Emma has taught us anything, it's that facing things head-on is best. Now I guess we have to put one foot in front of the other until we find a new kind of normal."

"Emma is the new normal and she comes first."

"That's for sure." His mother was emphatic.

"The thing is, Shelby is her mother. That means if you want to be a part of your granddaughter's life, you have to accept that fact." Donna started to say something and he held up a finger to stop her. "You also have to accept that she made the best choice available to her at the time. Can you do that?"

"If I have to." There was grudging acceptance in her voice.

Luke wasn't so sure about that but there was nothing he could do. Time would tell.

Right now he was concerned about something else. He'd never realized how well his mother knew him. That made him wonder what she meant about the way he'd looked at Shelby tonight. He shared a daughter with her pretty well but that didn't mean he trusted her.

He couldn't pretend anymore that he was neutral either. He wasn't angry, which was a blessing and curse. It had been all consuming, leaving no room for wanting her the way he had in the past. Now he wasn't mad and the longing sneaked in. Again.

He wanted Shelby, in his bed, up against the wall. Wherever, whenever. However he could have her. Trust wasn't required for sex and every time he saw her it took more willpower to keep from kissing her. Luke was afraid that's what his mother had seen in his eyes when he looked at Shelby. It was only a matter of time before Shelby saw it, too.

Chapter Ten

Shelby thought she couldn't be more nervous than she'd been facing Luke's mother for the first time since the woman had learned the truth. She'd been wrong. Several days later Donna McCoy had invited her to dinner next door and neither Luke nor Emma would be there. He'd explained that his mom wanted to talk without her granddaughter present so he took Emma to a movie. It was a daunting prospect to be alone with someone who hated her with the passion of a thousand suns. But she owed her a chance to have her say.

Carefully applying makeup and wearing her favorite jeans and white silky blouse with the navy blazer was the only armor she had for the battle ahead. She took one last look at herself in the mirror and nodded.

"She can say whatever she wants but words will bounce off," she said to her reflection. "Nothing can hurt you. It will all be over in a couple of hours."

Or sooner if things got too ugly. But Shelby was determined to let the woman get whatever she was feeling off her chest.

She went downstairs to tell her mother goodbye. Pam was in the kitchen reheating leftovers for dinner. After giving her the once-over, she said, "You look really nice, honey."

"Thanks."

There was a wistful, mushy expression on her mom's face. It was noteworthy because she always projected an aura of strength and rarely showed vulnerability. "Since you were a little girl, you always picked out your favorite outfit to wear when you had to do something that made you nervous."

"Best foot forward and all that."

Shelby tried to smile but her mouth trembled. So many emotions swirled inside her. This woman knew her from the inside out. Her mom had been harder on her than anyone and loved her more than anything.

"You don't have to go."

"That's tempting, but I have to."

"You don't owe her anything," Pam insisted.

"You're wrong about that, Mom. I owe her a chance to say whatever she has to." She met her mother's gaze. "If the situation was reversed, wouldn't you want a chance to be heard?"

"I suppose. Still—" The microwave beeped and Pam turned away to pull out the casserole she was reheating. "If it becomes too much, you don't have to stay and take it."

"Let's hope that doesn't happen." She looked at the digital clock on the stove. "It's time to go. Wish me luck."

Her mom moved closer and gave her a hug. Although she was affectionate to Emma all the time, spontaneous hugs for her daughter were rare. Did she feel guilty about her role in the sequence of events and decisions that kept Emma a secret from her father's family? Maybe. And for some reason believing Pam shared the burden gave her a little more strength to face what was to come.

"Thanks, Mom. I love you, too. See you later."

Shelby walked out the door and crossed the two driveways, then resolutely moved to the front porch next door. She rang the bell and waited while the nerves in her stomach jumped like drops of water in a hot skillet.

There were muted footsteps inside just before the door was opened and Donna stood there giving her a cool stare. "Shelby. I wasn't sure you'd actually come."

"To be honest, I didn't want to," she said. "But I accepted your invitation and here I am."

"Come in."

The politeness was stiff and forced, which made Shelby want to run in the other direction but she checked the impulse and trailed after the other woman to the kitchen. Delicious smells were coming from the oven and normally Shelby would have said something about it. Made innocuous conversation. But nothing about this situation was normal. It felt more like a visit to the principal's office for a chewing out followed by dispensation of punishment.

"How are you, Mrs. McCoy?"

"Fine."

Shelby hoped the woman would say more but it was a pipe dream at best. This was a consequence of her actions. But she was going to keep making idle conversation or die trying. "Are you enjoying your new home in Phoenix?"

"Yes."

Clipped, one-word responses designed to be hostile in the guise of civility. She had a sneaking suspicion the discomfort she felt was what a guy would experience when a woman was in a state of anger that was one step above the silent treatment. Luke's mother initiated this meeting but Shelby's stubborn streak kicked in. Call it a defense mechanism, but she could keep this up all night waiting for Donna to get to the point.

"It's been chilly here in California. How's the weather in Arizona?"

"Very pleasant."

Two words. That was progress. "Emma tells me

there's a pool and clubhouse in your housing development. She's looking forward to visiting you and going in the water."

The other woman stood on the other side of the island and glared. "Does she know how to swim?"

"Yes."

"I would know that if you had shared the fact that you had my son's child. I could have been a part of her life."

Each word was curt and sharp and pricked her guilt, drawing blood. She was determined not to let it show. "Yes, you would have. And you still can be in her life."

Donna lifted her hands in a helpless gesture. "That's all you have to say?"

"I'm here to let you dump on me. I know there's nothing I can say to make this better for you." Shelby rested a hand on the back of the bar stool beside her and stiffened her spine. "So, take your best shot, Mrs. McCoy."

"Okay." There was a flicker of something in the woman's dark eyes that could have been respect. "Emma came to my door once. I happened to be here getting it ready for new renters. She was selling holiday wrapping paper for a school fundraiser."

What? That was a shock. Emma wasn't supposed to go out alone and would certainly have been discouraged from coming over here. For obvious reasons. "She did?"

"I didn't buy anything." Her lips pressed together

for a moment. "If I'd known, I would have bought enough to make her the top seller in her class."

Shelby stayed quiet, sensing there was more to come.

"I don't know why that memory hurts so much more than anything else. It's just one of hundreds of missed opportunities."

"I know." Shelby easily recognized the guilt and remorse oozing through her.

"You and I were friends once, Shelby. You used to come over and talk to me." There was a different sort of hurt in the woman's eyes now.

"I remember," she said softly.

"When you and Luke started going out I was thrilled. You were so smart, so focused on high school and your grades for college. I hoped you would be a good influence on Luke."

"Yeah, I—"

"Until the other night I didn't know what broke the two of you up. At the time Luke didn't tell me anything, but I knew something was wrong with you two. He was on the edge more than I'd ever seen him. And you stopped dropping by."

"You believed I ended things," Shelby said.

The woman didn't answer, which was answer enough. "I missed seeing you. I wanted another child after Luke but it never happened. I'd hoped to have a girl. And for a while, with you, I felt what it must be like to have a daughter." She shook her head in frustration. "Now, to find out I have a granddaughter who was right here. I can't even put into words how that feels."

Shelby had promised herself she wouldn't say she was sorry anymore, but just this once she made an exception. "There's no way I can make it up to you, Mrs. Mac—" She stopped. Maybe it was being reminded of the friendship she'd had with this woman that made her use the nickname. Now it would just cause more anger and pain. "Mrs. McCoy, I'm sorry. More than you'll ever know and I'm well aware that it's too little too late. But I have to ask. Emma came to your door. You didn't suspect Luke was her father?"

"I didn't rent the house out until a few months after Luke went into the army. While I was still here, I saw another boy coming to your house. More than once."

"There's no reason you should believe this, but I didn't sleep around. And I was pregnant with Emma, although not showing yet. If someone came over it was about school." Her tone had turned defensive so she forced a calmness into her voice when she said, "I don't mean this to be confrontational. That's the last thing I want. I'm the only one who has responsibility for this. But Luke saw the resemblance instantly. Is it possible you didn't want to know? Because then you would have to say something. And Luke was successful in the army. His relationship with you was troubled. Maybe you didn't want to rock the boat?"

"Luke had a right to know and so did I."

"You're not wrong. I can't argue with that." Shelby looked down for a moment. "If I were you, I wouldn't care about this but I have to say it anyway. I was seventeen, Mrs. McCoy. I was pregnant and terrified I would be out on the street. I wasn't thinking about ten years into the future or who else might be affected. My body was changing and there was no way everyone wouldn't know I was going to have a baby. I saw judgment everywhere I looked."

"Shelby—"

"All I could think about was how in the world was I going to take care of a baby when I couldn't even take care of myself. It felt as if I would always be seventeen and scared."

The other woman sighed. "Luke said your mother didn't want you to tell him about the baby."

"That's true. She thought she was doing the right thing," Shelby defended. "But I was going to tell him anyway. Before I could he said he'd joined the army."

She looked away for a moment. "He told me."

"You have no reason to believe this either, but I realized not saying anything was best for Luke. He'd been restless and looking for something. He was pulling his life together and I didn't want to mess that up for him. I wanted to help and the best way to do that was to let him go."

"Now here we are," his mom said.

"Yes."

"Would you like a glass of wine?"

The offer was unexpected even though the open bottle was right there on the island. Shelby glanced at it. "I would. More than you can possibly imagine."

"Me, too. It's been breathing awhile." She poured the red liquid into the two tumblers beside the bottle then handed one over. "Luke keeps wine here for you."

Shelby couldn't believe that was true, but figured saying nothing was prudent.

The other woman took a sip from her glass, then said, "Did you know why Luke broke things off with you?"

"Not then." Shelby's eyes widened as the revelation sank in. "I thought he was just over me. That he didn't care the way I—" She shook her head. "I just thought I was a fling and he was bored."

His mother smiled for the first time but it was sad around the edges. "You two remind me of that Christmas story about the husband who sells his watch to buy a comb for his wife. And she sells her hair to buy a chain for his watch. You each sacrificed for the other. Protecting each other."

All the pain and rejection she'd felt when he broke things off came rushing back to her now. Things could have been so different. "I wish he'd said something to me. Look, Mrs. McCoy—"

"Call me Donna," she said. "Mrs. Mac makes me feel a hundred years old. And you're all grown up now."

"Okay. Donna—" Shelby tested out the sound of

that and felt a little weird. "I know I can't make all of this up to you. But I will do my best to help you get to know Emma better. You can see her all the time. I won't keep her from you."

"I appreciate that." Donna's voice had softened and the resentment seemed to be fading a little. "Luke says I'm still processing all of this. And I appreciate you being willing and brave enough to talk to me."

"It's the least I can do."

"There's a lot of truth in what you said," the woman acknowledged. "It will take some time, but I'm sure eventually I'll find acceptance."

"Whatever I can do to help. All you have to do is ask," Shelby said.

She saw more of the woman who had once been her friend. There wasn't complete absolution in her words but the foundation for it was there. And then she had a déjà vu moment. Her first thought was to tell Luke about this. In the past, anything good or bad that happened to her she'd shared first with him. Happiness and relief that she and his mom had made peace gave way to sadness because it was a painful reminder.

The past was gone. Luke would never again be her first, best confidant. Not her lover, or her love.

Luke had spent his day off painting the living room. The roller made covering the walls go pretty fast but the finishing work was tedious. Baseboards and doors needed a brush and lots of patience. The job looked good but he didn't take as much satisfaction from it as he'd expected. And now he was tired but oddly restless. Hungry but didn't feel like eating.

He recalled this feeling from years ago when he was conflicted about what to do with his life. The common denominator between then and now was Shelby. Then he'd made the decision to break up with her but now they were co-parenting. Emma was all they had in common. He was her father and there was no breaking up from that, even if he wanted to.

But he kept waiting for the pesky attraction to his child's mother to go away. Now he figured when he sold the house and moved he'd leave the feelings behind. It was just about her being next door again. Some sense of déjà vu.

His stomach growled, reminding him that he should eat. His mom had cooked and frozen individual meals for him, which he appreciated. It felt good to resolve their differences and put the past to rest. She'd left a couple of days ago and Luke actually missed her, something that hadn't seemed possible when he went into the army.

He pulled a container labeled "pork chop in mushroom sauce" out of the freezer. She'd even written reheating instructions with a Sharpie on a piece of tape.

"Thanks, Ma," he said to the empty room.

He put the food in the microwave and pushed the reheat button. Over the humming microwave there was a sound, like a tapping on the sliding glass door, but it was past eight and dark outside. All his instincts went on high alert when he turned but Shelby was standing there. She lifted her hand in a small wave.

There was a twisting sensation in his chest that he wished he could pin on being hungry but that was a stretch. Then his head cleared and anxiety sliced through him. Emma.

Quickly he moved to the door, unlocked it and slid the glass open. "Is Emma okay?"

"Define okay." She looked frazzled then said, "Physically she's fine. But she's nine and really good at it."

"Oh?"

"She's been pestering me to wear lipstick. Can you believe that? Like I said, she's nine."

"You said no." It wasn't a question.

"I did. Emphatically. See, that's the thing. She doesn't accept no. There isn't any part of that word she understands. She won't let this go and it's like being pecked to death by a chicken."

"So you abandoned ship."

"Yes." She pointed a warning finger at him. "And if she asks you, it's a negative on her wearing lipstick, or any other makeup."

"Understood." He nodded. "Where is she now?"

"I sent her to her room to read herself to sleep. If she comes out before morning to do anything besides go to the bathroom, there will be dire consequences," Shelby vowed. "Before coming over I checked and she was asleep."

Luke realized she was still standing outside. "Would you like to come in?"

"I thought you'd never ask."

She smiled and the dimple in her cheek flashed. There was a time when he was a sucker for that smile and the sweet innocence in her eyes. Not anymore. Probably. She walked past him and moved over to the kitchen island, but the tempting scent of her skin lingered and filled his senses.

After taking a seat in one of the chairs, she met his gaze. "This is where I ask if your mom is right about you keeping wine here for me."

"She told you that?"

"Yes." Shelby had a spark of mischief in her eyes.

His mom had accused him of doing that but he'd denied it, sidestepped her question and never admitted anything. Obviously she knew him better than he'd realized because he did have a nice red on hand and Shelby might have mentioned that it was her favorite. Beer or scotch were his alcoholic beverages of choice, not wine.

"I have some," was all he said. "I'd be a pretty bad detective if I didn't figure out that you'd like a glass."

"The bad guys better watch their backs. Detective McCoy is on the job."

That teasing reminded him of Emma. The kid might look like him, but her voice, mannerisms and sense of humor were all Shelby. And this woman was even more beautiful than the girl who'd confounded and charmed him years ago.

Luke still didn't have wineglasses. Even though it seemed he'd been pouring a lot lately there didn't seem much point in buying them. That would be more to move when the time came.

He got out the inelegant tumbler and poured cabernet into it. "Here you go."

"Thanks." She took a sip of the ruby liquid then looked at him. "So your mom got home okay?"

"Yeah."

"How was the visit?"

"Good." He got a cold beer, then took the chair beside hers at the island. "Better than I expected."

"Why was that?" she asked, shifting in the seat.

Her shoulder brushed his and he felt that twist in his chest again. *Ignore it. Doesn't mean anything.* What did she just say? Right. She was asking how things went with his mom's visit. "In the past there was always tension and drama with us."

Shelby met his gaze. "So no drama this time?"

"No, there was drama but not about me. We discussed the past and cleared the air. Turns out most of our differences were generated by her being a good mom who was worried about me." He toyed with the cold beer bottle in front of him. "With a lot of maturity and being a father now, I understand where she was coming from."

"Being a parent does change one's perspective," she said thoughtfully. "That small human we made makes you feel so many things—anxiety, responsibility, pride, unconditional love. And I don't think anyone on the planet can exasperate you more than a child. Or a parent."

"Speaking of that, how did things go with you and my mom?"

Shelby looked surprised. "Donna didn't tell you?"

"I didn't ask. So it's Donna now?" he teased. "I guess that's something. And she was in a pretty good mood when Emma and I got home from the movie."

"That's a good sign." Shelby took a sip from her glass, then held it between her hands. "She was understandably upset with me for not telling her about Emma and didn't hold back. I shared my reasons, all of which you already know."

"Yeah."

"Speaking of knowing stuff…" She glanced sideways at him. "She and I talked about you breaking up with me and why."

"Hmm."

"She thinks we should have been more open and honest with each other." There were questions in her eyes.

"Remind me to have a talk with my mom about her high-level clearance and being more selective about what information she shares."

"Shuttle diplomacy comes to mind," Shelby said wryly. "Anyway, I think we're in a better place than we were. She's a good person and wants to be a part of Emma's life. I encourage that. We all want the best for our girl, after all. Even my mom, although—"

"What is it? You were frazzled when you knocked

on my door. I'm sensing it wasn't just about Emma."
He took a long drink of his beer. "Am I right?"

"Yes. No. Maybe." She sighed. "You might as well
know. You're going to hear sooner or later."

"What? Should I be worried?"

"No. I contacted an attorney about putting your
name on Emma's birth certificate."

"Oh?" He had to give her points for following
through on the promise.

"It was my omission in the first place and it's only
right for me to take responsibility and correct things.
I could do it myself, but the lawyer will make sure
it's done right." She shrugged.

"And your mom is opposed."

"She doesn't like change, no matter that it won't
alter anything. But your rights should be protected,
spelled out. For medical decisions. Or custody if anything happens to me. God forbid there's anything
serious. Ever. But there shouldn't be any question."

"Nothing's going to happen to you." *He wouldn't
let it.* The thought popped into his mind before he
could stop it. As if he had anything to say about her
future. A long time ago he might have but that ship
had sailed.

"From your mouth to God's ear." She smiled at
him. "But there are no guarantees."

"I know. Odds are against it though."

"That's interesting coming from you. A cop.
Law enforcement is necessary because bad stuff
happens." She frowned. "Now that I think about it,

you're on defense against all the bad stuff that happens. Should I be nervous?"

"My job isn't dangerous. I interview people and gather facts, statements, information from crime scenes that will be evidence to make a case in a court of law. Don't worry. It's not like what you see on TV."

"I can't help worrying. Tell me what you did today."

The concern on her face made him feel good at the same time he wanted to reassure her. "Today I painted the living room and was in more danger from the fumes than anything I do on the street. Before you ask, yesterday I arrested a B&E—breaking and entering—suspect who was operating in a seniors neighborhood."

"That's awful. Preying on older people. Good for you getting him off the street."

"Shucks, ma'am. Just doing my job." It had felt good, though. Almost as good as it felt when she looked at him as if he was a hero. Like now. He could get used to this feeling and decided to change the subject. "What did you do today?"

"I had an awesome day, actually." She smiled and swiveled her chair toward him, her knees grazing his thigh. "There's this student, a boy. So smart, so surly and rebellious. But I'm determined to help him see his potential whether he wants to or not."

"How?"

"I talk to him. About his less than ideal family situation, how smart he is, how much I believe in him. And today he had a breakthrough." She was excited

and her legs were still touching his. "I've been trying to make math fun for the kids."

"Good luck with that."

"You're such a pessimist." But her enthusiasm
didn't fade. "I created activities based on TV game
shows. This kid is super competitive. Today he won
the match. My favorite juvenile delinquent won the
gift card for a fast-food place all the kids like."

"Is he a troublemaker?" Her safety concerned
him.

"No. It's a shell, an act. Apparently I have a soft
spot for that type, but I see through him. He's a really
good kid." She leaned forward and put her hand on
his arm. "Not unlike someone else I used to know."

Luke remembered when no one but her saw the
good in him. She had been the calm in the storm that
was his life. Light to his darkness and he hadn't been
able to resist her then.

Or now apparently. Their faces were so close and
he couldn't stop himself. He kissed her. She tasted
like wine but the softness of her lips was the same.
It felt as if no time had passed. Felt like the first time
when he surprised her. She'd leaned in then, too, and
her breathing wasn't so even anymore.

Unlike last time she pulled away first and
wouldn't quite meet his gaze. "Luke, I—"

"Shelby, that was—" He dragged his fingers
through his hair. "I was feeling nostalgic, I guess."

"Right. Of course." She swiveled her knees away
and slid off the chair. "For old times' sake. That's all."

"Yeah. We haven't seen each other for ten years.

Just a stroll down memory lane. It was bound to happen."

"Yup. I was feeling nostalgic, too." Her cheeks were flushed and she was still a little breathless.

His body was feeling more than nostalgia because grinding need churned through him. It had never been more clear to him how a guy's body disconnected from his brain. Because when he started to think clearly again, he couldn't understand why he kissed this woman who had lied to him. Could he rationalize that away and call it gratitude for her protecting his paternal rights?

"Anyway—" She moved around the island to the sliding glass door. "I need to go. Get back and check on Emma. And I didn't say anything to my mom about leaving the house. She could be wondering where I am."

And Pam wouldn't be happy she was here to unload her feelings.

"Okay."

"Thanks for the wine. And the whine." She grinned. "Good night, Luke."

Then she was gone. He blew out a breath and realized his dinner was still in the microwave and he'd forgotten all about being restless. Because of Shelby? No way. Of all the women on the planet, he wouldn't let her be the antidote to his tension.

Chapter Eleven

For the next few days Shelby thought of time in terms of her life before the kiss and after. She had trouble concentrating on her students, her lesson plans and her daughter because the feel of Luke's lips on hers was never far from her mind.

Why did he do it? What had he been thinking? *Had* he been thinking? Of payback or torture? Kissing him felt like either or both because she'd liked it so much and there wasn't a snowball's chance in hell of it going anywhere.

Thank goodness today was Saturday and she didn't have to think or make decisions. It was cleaning day in her world and she welcomed mindless physical work. Thoughts of that kiss still scrolled through her mind while she scrubbed the upstairs bathtub but only her hormones were affected. And possibly her imagination was in overdrive but there was a good chance that the bathroom had never sparkled quite so brightly when she finished.

Her back on the other hand was begging for a break. Shelby stowed the cleaning supplies and grabbed the can of spray wax and a cloth for dusting. Walking down the upstairs hall toward her room, she passed Emma's and saw her daughter playing with dolls. The carpet was littered with clothes, most of which belonged to the nine-year-old, not the doll. The bed was unmade and books were scattered over it.

"Emma Rose, what are you doing?"

Dark eyes, Luke's eyes, stared innocently back at her. "I had to change my doll's outfit."

"That's more important than cleaning your room?"

Emma looked around at the chaos and glanced at the iPad beside her. "It's not that bad."

"Not that bad—" Shelby stopped and took a breath. This was a familiar argument. She didn't want to overreact because of being on edge about Luke's kiss and trying to make sense of what it meant. "Saturday is always cleaning day. This is not new. On this day I expect your room to be neat as a pin. The other six days of the week it can look like a barn, but not today. I don't think that's unreasonable."

"I'll do it, Mommy. As soon as I get around to it."

Shelby felt her irritation crank up a notch and prayed for patience. Children learned what they lived and sometimes it was like looking in a mirror. She'd probably said that to Emma more than she realized.

"I'll give you ten minutes to finish what you're doing, then I'm coming back to check that you've started your chores."

"Okay, Mommy." She didn't look up.

Shelby went to her room to dust and declutter. Her desk was littered with papers—math homework to correct, school memos and mail. She had a file with legal paperwork to change her daughter's name to Emma Rose Richards McCoy.

After sorting through and organizing everything there were still stacks, but orderly ones. On the bench at the foot of her bed she'd thrown a pair of worn jeans and a long-sleeved white T-shirt, the clothes she'd had on when she saw Luke the other night.

She picked up the shirt and pressed her nose into it and swore she could smell his scent in the material. An ache started deep in her belly, a yearning to be in his arms. To kiss him until she could forget about how they'd hurt each other and just be snuggled against him without a care in the world. But wishing for what could never be was a new kind of pain.

"Mommy!" Emma rushed into her room, cheeks flushed with excitement.

"What, sweetie? Is your room clean?" She tossed the shirt into her clothes hamper.

"I just got a message from Karen."

Shelby knew it came on Emma's iPad. It had a kid-friendly message app and parents could control who had access to communicate with their child. This was a way to give her a little freedom in a responsible way.

"What did she want?"

Emma looked up eagerly. "She's going to the mall with some girls in our class and wants me to come."

"Is her mom taking you?"

"Yes. Then she's going to do errands and will come back to get us." The little girl pressed her hands together in a pleading gesture. "Can I go, Mom? Please?"

There were all kinds of red flags in the scenario she'd just proposed. At nine Emma wasn't sophisticated enough to filter her words and Shelby dreaded a time when she would.

"So, Karen's mom isn't staying with you at the mall?"

"There will be a lot of us." Emma didn't exactly answer the question but her enthusiasm dimmed. "We'll stay together."

"But there won't be adult supervision, right?"

"We'll be fine, Mommy."

"I'm not comfortable with this arrangement, Em. I think a grown-up should be with you."

"But I'm nine! Almost ten."

Shelby could see rebellion in her little girl's expression and body language and wondered if this was how Luke had looked when he got a no from his mom. "You are nine. But I can't always count on you to be responsible."

"I'll clean my room before I go," Emma promised.

Shelby wanted to say she rested her case but this child wouldn't understand what she meant. "I know you're growing up, sweetie, but I don't think you're old enough yet to go there by yourselves." When Emma opened her mouth to protest Shelby said, "That's my final answer."

Since when did being a mother make her sound like a contestant on a TV game show?

"You're just mean." The little girl vibrated with self-righteous indignation. "I'm going to ask my dad. He'll say yes."

That was a first. Before Shelby could fully process this new development, Emma marched out of the room and down the stairs. She had time to send Luke a quick warning text before hurrying after her daughter.

Emma was waiting on Luke's porch when Shelby caught up to her. He answered the door looking all masculine in paint-splattered jeans and a snug, stained T-shirt that highlighted the muscles in his arms and the contours of his chest. But Shelby didn't have time to swoon. In a little girl's world hearing the word *no* was equivalent to the end of the world.

"Hi." He looked at her then his daughter. "What's up?"

"She won't let me go to the mall," Emma complained. "Tell her it's okay."

Shelby was torn between wanting to present her arguments for the decision she'd made and holding back to see just how Luke would handle this situation. She decided to observe.

"Why don't you come inside and we'll talk about this." He stepped back and held the door wide-open for them.

Points to him for a cooling off strategy, Shelby thought.

The living room was full of paint paraphernalia, although it was looking good. But this wasn't the time to say so and she silently followed him to the kitchen.

"Can I get either of you something to drink?"

"No—" A beat went by before Emma added, "thank you."

"Shelby?" he said.

"Nothing, thanks."

He rested his hands on his hips and looked at both of them before asking, "So what's going on?"

Emma jumped in. "My friend Karen wants me to go to the mall with her and some other girls. Mommy said no."

He met Shelby's gaze then said to the little girl, "Your mom must have had a reason, right?"

"Not a good one." She folded her arms over her thin chest.

He waited for more but she didn't elaborate. "Are you going to tell me why she won't let you go?"

Emma shifted her feet a little nervously and glanced away. "Karen's mom is dropping us off."

"So you girls will be there alone?" He frowned.

Reluctantly Emma said, "Yes, but we stay together. It's safe."

Luke's eyebrows pulled together and his frown deepened as the situation became clearer. "Emma, I wish I could say yes, but I agree with your mom about this. Unless an adult is with you girls the whole time, I don't think it's okay for you to be there by yourselves."

The little girl's expression turned tragic for a moment, then she had an idea because there was a glimmer of hope in her eyes. "You could go with us. You're grown up and a policeman."

Again Shelby could have run interference. After all he was wearing the evidence to support a negative response. But the look on his face was priceless. She'd pay big bucks to see Luke McCoy shepherd a group of nine-year-old girls around the mall. Judging by the shock and surprise she now saw, he'd rather take a sharp stick to the eye.

"Honey," he finally said, "I'm full of paint. Today isn't a good day. But we can plan another time—"

"I want to go today." Her tone was in the stubborn and unreasonable range.

"Then I have to say no." Luke sounded as if turning her down was killing him. "I agree with your mom."

Emma glared at both of them, a look that could

have reduced lesser parents to a brown stain on the sidewalk. "I don't like you guys very much right now."

Luke reached out a paint-covered hand. "Em, listen—"

But she'd already turned away and walked out the front door. He looked as if she'd cut his heart out and started to go after her.

Now Shelby jumped in. She put her hand on his arm and it felt sticky. Even the contact with paint didn't diminish the thrill of touching him. "Let her go. You can't reason with her right now."

There was misery in his eyes when he looked at her. "That was the single hardest thing I've ever done. Second hardest was telling her no on that sleepover the first time she spent the night here."

"And that worked out okay," she pointed out.

"Because you marched her back here and made her apologize."

"And she got over it, right?" Shelby reminded him.

"But why does the right call feel so wrong? I'm sure you noticed that she doesn't like us very much."

"She's been warned about saying she hates anyone so the good news is she didn't do that." Shelby sighed. "I wish I could say it gets easier, but that would be a lie. On the upside—"

"Is there one?"

"Yeah. This is the first time I've ever had someone to back me up."

"What about your mom?" he asked.

"She gives in and spoils Em on the simple stuff. The harder decisions the best she can manage is neutral which isn't the same as supporting me. I appreciate your cooperation."

"It was a no-brainer. Little girls at the mall. No adult." He shuddered. "There are so many scenarios where that goes sideways in a hurry."

"I know." Shelby's phone vibrated and she pulled it out of her jeans pocket and read the text message. "Karen's mom just found out about this mall trip and is a hard no, too. I didn't have a chance to check with her before Em came running to you. We wouldn't have had to bother you if she'd waited a few minutes."

"I would have preferred to skip this, but it's no bother. I'm her dad. That means being a part of her life for the good, bad, ugly."

Shelby smiled. "And now I know you're made of sterner stuff."

"It sure doesn't feel that way," he said, shaking his head.

"Don't worry, Luke. She'll get over it."

"Promise?" There was a gleam in his eyes now, chasing away the agony of having to say no to his daughter.

"I absolutely do." She checked him out from head to toe. "You look like you've gone a couple of rounds with the paint and it's winning."

"Not my favorite chore, but it gave me an excuse to get out of being a mall cop."

"Yeah, that went through my mind, too." Shelby laughed, then wandered over to the doorway to check out the room he'd finished. "This looks really good. You've done a fantastic job. The color is perfect."

"I like it, too." And when he looked down at her his eyes were smoldering with the same expression he'd worn the other night just before he kissed her.

Shelby's heart started to race and her pulse jumped. She had the most absurd desire to pull that T-shirt off him and check out where the paint hadn't touched his skin. It was time to get the heck out of there.

"I better go deal with the fallout. If luck is on my side Emma has already heard about the busted plan from Karen." Without looking at him again she headed for the door. "Thanks for your help, Luke."

"Anytime."

She hurried back to her house and ducked into the downstairs bathroom so her cheeks would cool before facing Emma or her mom. Why were life situations always good news and bad? For the first time she had someone to back her up in this adventure called parenthood. It worked out with them being in agreement. But what if he disagreed? That was the bad part. She would have to listen to him whether or not she wanted to. They might have to compromise in order to present a united front which was crucial.

Also crucial was figuring out just why Luke had

kissed her. There was no reason to do it because he'd made it clear they would work together for Emma but he would never trust or forgive her. Without that there could be nothing more between them. No second chances, no matter how much she might wish otherwise.

A few days after telling Emma no, Luke pulled into his driveway after work and saw her on his doorstep. He glanced next door, automatically looking for Shelby but saw her mother instead. The woman didn't even pretend not to be standing guard when he met her gaze, but folded her arms over her chest and stared daggers. That wasn't creepy at all.

He got out of the truck and started to walk toward the house but his daughter ran to meet him with a hug. He hadn't seen her since her mall meltdown and was relieved that she wasn't holding a grudge. Far from it, apparently.

This was the best and he could get used to someone greeting him like this after a long day. Shelby's pretty face flashed into his mind and made him want a hug and kiss from her, too. Obviously the empty feeling he'd carried around for so long was only half filled by his child.

"Hey, kid, what's up?"

"Daddy, do you have a flashlight? With batteries that aren't dead?"

"Yes. Why?"

"It's for my science project. Me and mommy have to make a rainbow. Ours doesn't work."

"Your rainbow?" he teased.

"No, our flashlight, silly." She grinned. "Mommy is grading papers and can't go get batteries until she's finished. I've been waiting forever for you to get home from work."

He'd learned that when you're nine forever can be five minutes. "Well, I'm here now. Let's go find that flashlight."

Luke unlocked his door and opened it to let her in. "Look in the kitchen drawers, Em. I'm going upstairs to change."

"Okay."

Just before he walked into his room, he heard her say, "Found it. I'll see if it works." *It won't for long if you play with it*, he thought. But there was something about turning that handheld light off and on that was irresistible to a kid. He remembered doing it, then getting the warning from his dad about not having light when you really needed it. After putting on jeans and a navy T-shirt with HHPD in white letters on the back, he jogged back down the stairs.

There was a light going on and off in the kitchen and he grinned. He didn't have the heart to stop her. The mall decision had to be a no. Playing with the flashlight not so much. He would just stock up on batteries.

"I found it, Daddy," she said when he walked into the kitchen.

"You sure did. Is there anything else you need?"

Her little face scrunched into a thoughtful expression. "I don't think so."

"Did you have dinner yet?"

"A little while ago," she said. "Roast, mashed potatoes. And carrots. They're not as bad as broccoli."

He laughed. After a day spent investigating criminal complaints she was a breath of fresh air. "I can see how that would be the case."

"I'm going to see if Mommy is finished working." She started to turn away, then stopped. "Do you want to come over and help us make a rainbow?"

All he had to do was look at her. She was bright and shiny and full of color. He wanted to spend as much time as possible with her. Seeing Shelby, too, was a bigger plus than he wanted it to be. Grammy might not approve of him being there but right this second he would walk through the fires of hell to spend time with Emma and Shelby.

"I would love to help." He felt as if he'd handed her the moon when she smiled from ear to ear.

Emma grabbed his hand and tugged him toward the front door. "Let's go."

"Let's take the shortcut?"

Her eyes went wide with excitement when she looked up. "You mean through the back fence?"

"Yes." He angled his head toward the sliding glass door. It was an unexpected joy to share the secret of the shortcut between the houses with the next generation. "Lead the way, kid."

After turning on the outside light to illuminate the backyard, Luke followed his daughter to the loose board in the fence. "Your mom and I used to go back and forth to each other's houses through here when we were kids."

"Were you nine?"

"Older than that." He didn't want to tell her about climbing up on the patio cover and sneaking into Shelby's room for a kiss. "I'll lift the board for you. Be careful."

She slipped through easily. It was wide but he had to maneuver his shoulders to fit. It was tighter than when he was younger. That wasn't the only change. He had a daughter now and their budding relationship had survived telling her no. She turned his heart into a gooey mess every time he saw her. They'd come a long way in a short time and he had Shelby to thank for it. That did a lot to cancel out his resentment. It had been the only thing standing in the way of him kissing her. Now that he had, he wanted more.

Emma tried to open the sliding glass door at her house and couldn't move it. "It's locked I think."

"We'll knock. If no one hears, we'll go to the front door."

"Okay."

Her little fist didn't make very much noise so he rapped his knuckles on the glass. A few moments later Pam appeared in the kitchen. She saw Emma and looked relieved. He got a disapproving frown but she unlocked the slider and opened it.

"Emma Rose, I was worried about you."

"Why? You watched me go over to Daddy's."

Luke knew he was the core of her grandmother's worry and was curious about how she would explain this.

"You were gone for a long time. I just—I was waiting for you out front."

"Daddy and me took the shortcut through the fence."

Pam didn't look happy, then she noticed the flashlight. "So you got what you needed."

"Yes. I'm going to see if Mommy is finished with her work and can help me now. I'll be right back."

Luke watched her walk out of the room and said, "I'll be right here."

"Will you?" Pam said softly.

"Will I what?" He knew Emma loved this woman and would never say anything negative when she was around. But anger hummed through him proving he wasn't over his resentment for her grandmother. She'd manipulated her vulnerable daughter and cost him years with his. "What's your problem?"

"You are," she confirmed. "I keep waiting for you to leave Shelby and Emma. To hurt them."

"So you can say 'I told you so'?"

"It's your pattern, not sticking around."

He noticed she didn't deny his accusation. "You should know that I'm not going away."

"Not entirely true. You're going to sell the house after fixing it up."

"All that means is I won't be next door. I'm not leaving Huntington Hills."

"Not yet." Her lips thinned and accusation burned in her eyes. "But it's just a matter of time until you do."

"That's not fair. When I left for the army I didn't have all the facts. And you're the one to blame for that."

"Shelby made the decision."

"The decision she made was because of pressure you put on her," he shot back.

"I'm her mother."

"And I'm Emma's father. I will always be there for her."

"If you say so." Pam's tone said that, in her opinion, there was zero chance he'd keep that promise.

Time would prove he was telling the truth. "You'll see."

"See what?" Shelby walked into the room holding Emma's hand.

"How this whole rainbow experiment thing goes." He studied her expression to see if she'd sensed the tension in the room but couldn't tell one way or the other. Maybe he'd pulled off the pivot.

"I showed Mommy your flashlight and she said it's perfect."

"Good."

"Emma said you just got home from work. Did you have dinner?" Shelby asked.

"Didn't have time what with rainbows to make." He shrugged.

"We would have waited for you to eat," she protested. "You must be starving."

Luke glanced at her mom. He wouldn't put it past her to cut him off at the knees and didn't want to miss out on this. He wanted to stay as long as possible. "I know you run a tight ship and this has to be done before bedtime. It's getting late and I didn't want to keep her up."

"I'll reheat something for you," Shelby said. "We're okay on time."

Pam looked as if she'd swallowed a lemon but apparently shared his sentiment about not being negative in front of Emma. "I'm going upstairs."

"But, Grammy, you'll miss the rainbow."

"You can show me in the morning before school." The woman kissed the little face. "Good night, love."

"Night, Grammy."

After she left it was the three of them. Just like that contentment and satisfaction filled up that hollow place inside Luke. Maybe for the first time ever.

Shelby took out a plate and filled it with roast, mashed potatoes, gravy and the dreaded carrots. She put it in the microwave with a plastic cover and punched in the reheat command on the front of the appliance.

She smiled. "In three to five minutes your stomach will be much happier."

He looked at her, then his daughter and realized he was already happy. "Smells good."

"While Daddy is eating, I'll get out what we need," Emma said.

"Okay. Computer paper is upstairs and we have glasses in here in the cupboard." She noticed the flashlight in her daughter's hand. "Leave that here so you don't use up the batteries. We'll be right back where we started."

"Daddy didn't tell me I couldn't turn it on."

Shelby gave him a look that said she knew he'd been spineless and why. "Well, I'm telling you. Now put it on the table."

"O-okay." She reluctantly did as ordered and left the room.

The microwave beeped and Shelby removed the plate then set it on the table. "Dinner is served."

"Thanks." He sat down and she handed him a knife, fork and napkin. As the mouthwatering smells filled the room he realized how hungry he was and dug into the food. "This is really good."

"I'm glad you like it."

As he was finishing up, Emma returned with an eight-and-a-half-by-eleven-inch piece of white computer paper. She put it on the table beside him.

"Now I need a glass of water. Can you get it, Mommy? I can't reach."

"Sure." Shelby pulled a glass out of the cupboard

and put tap water in before setting it on the paper. "Now you can turn on the flashlight. Shine it through the water."

The little girl did as instructed. "Look! There's a rainbow on the paper!"

"Water is made up of colors also known as wavelengths," Shelby explained. "It's reflection, refraction and dispersion of light. Parallel lines, circles and arcs. The set of points which appear bright form an arc. The rainbow appears to have different colors because the colors that make up the light have different angles of deflection."

"Huh?" Emma looked confused.

"Way to take the joy out of a rainbow." Luke grinned.

"What?" Shelby shrugged. "That's the scientific explanation. You can't go wrong with math."

"She's nine," he said wryly. "I'm a lot older than that and my brain wanted to explode."

Emma held up the flashlight with two hands. "It's really pretty."

"Yeah." But Luke wasn't looking at the rainbow.

He couldn't take his eyes off Shelby. He couldn't resist teasing her but she made smart look sexy as hell. More than ever he wanted to kiss her again and go where that took them. That was a problem with a capital *P*.

He'd told her mother that he was going to be around for his daughter. His life and Shelby's would always be linked and that made these feelings tangled and torturous. Every time he saw her the urge to have her was more powerful. How was he going to stop himself from taking a step that would make everything even more complicated?

She'd fed him dinner, but he was still hungry. For her.

Chapter Twelve

Shelby was pacing in her bedroom, restless after making rainbows. It went well thanks to Luke for providing the flashlight. Her problem now was that he'd provided a lot more than that. Nothing tangible that she could simply return to him because her life was nothing if not complicated.

He'd gone home but left her with a yearning that was unlike anything she'd ever felt before. Or maybe it had always been there for him and after he left for the army she'd just ignored the longing, or covered it up with a heaping helping of denial.

Now she couldn't pretend the ache wasn't there. Now she had to face it. When he was here earlier helping with Emma's project, Shelby had a hard time keeping her hands to herself. A long time ago the most natural thing in the world had been touching Luke and she wanted to again. Rub his broad, strong back. Rest her fingers on his forearm. It was like putting a box of donuts in front of a sweets-obsessed dieter. She had never been reckless or rebellious. Always the good girl doing the right thing. Luke had been her only revolt and that was ten years ago. She was about to start the next decade with another one.

She stopped pacing and looked out the window. If his house was dark she would just let it go and part of her prayed the lights were off. They weren't.

She pulled her cell phone from her slacks pocket and typed in a message then texted it to Luke.

You awake?

Moments later there was a response. Yes. You? That was followed by a smiley face emoji.

She messaged back. It's late and okay for you to say no. Feel like company?

She waited and the response took longer this time. Just when she was about to tell him never mind, her phone vibrated with his response. Come on over. Through the fence.

On my way.

Shelby turned off the lights in her room, walked out into the hall, then closed the door. She checked on Emma, who was sound asleep, before creeping over to her mom's bedroom door. After listening for a few moments she heard no sound which meant the TV was off and that was usually a sign that she was asleep. Even if she wasn't, Pam didn't normally bother her during the night.

Quietly Shelby went downstairs to the kitchen, opened the sliding glass door, then slipped outside. She stealthily moved across the patio, into the grass and walked halfway down the length of the fence to where the loose board was located. Luke was already there holding it up for her to step through.

He put a finger to his lips, pointed to the house and indicated she should follow him. Without a word she did. In his kitchen she let out a long breath.

Grinning, Luke said, "Just like the good old days."

"Not quite. Then it was *you* sneaking into *my* house," she reminded him.

"So you are sneaking, then." He folded his arms over his chest and his expression gave no clue what he was thinking. Cop face. "You didn't tell your mom where you were going."

"No. She's asleep." Probably.

He nodded and said, "Would you like a glass of wine?"

"No. Thanks. But feel free to have a beer if you want one."

He shook his head and indicated the small dinette nearby. "Do you want to sit? It's either here or at the island."

"The table is new."

He shrugged. "I got it for Emma. Seemed—better."

"New table it is." She sat and looked at him, her heart beating a little too fast. "Maybe I will have wine."

"Coming right up."

She watched him get out the glass and the wine and pour it before grabbing a beer and bringing drinks over. Then he set them on the table and sat at a right angle to her. He took a sip from his drink before cradling the bottle between his hands, as if he needed to keep them occupied.

"So, what's on your mind?" he asked.

"How did you know—" She stopped before the stupid question could come out of her mouth. "I'm not in the habit of coming to see you so late. Obviously there's something."

"Is it Emma?"

"In a way. I think I know the answer to this question, but I have to ask." She met his gaze. "Did you mind that she came to you to borrow the flashlight, then dragged you over to be involved in her science assignment?"

His response was swift, decisive and adamant. "No. Why would you even question that?"

"I don't know. Probably because I've been doing this parenting thing alone for so long. It's hard to not be the primary person in Emma's life anymore. It's not that I'm unwilling to share her. I hope you know that. But the single mom habit is firmly entrenched. I want to assure you that if I forget to invite you in I'm not intentionally leaving you out."

"Understood."

"Eventually it will be the new kind of normal. Just like you said."

"I thought you were good with me backing you up," he said.

"I am. It's just—" She sighed. "This is where I tell you that I'm probably crazy and should have my head examined. But when Em wanted to go to the mall and I told her no, that should have been the end of it. And until you that would have been. But she wanted a second opinion."

"And I agreed with your decision."

"What if you hadn't?" she asked.

"I'm a cop, Shelby. I know better than anyone that little girls and boys go missing every day from malls and other public places. As far as parenting decisions go, that was probably the easiest one we'll ever have to make." He looked at her. "Don't get me wrong. I don't like telling her no and probably never will. But it had to be done."

"Right. But sometimes there's a lot of gray area. Like wearing lipstick."

"Hard no. Like you said. She's nine."

"Or how old she has to be to get a cell phone. I can hear the argument now. 'All my friends have one why can't I?' She just spits out whatever pops into her head and it doesn't matter which one of us she's with."

"Then we have to start practicing this phrase— 'Let me think about it.' Or variations on that theme. Then we discuss the request together and come up with an answer."

"You make it all sound so easy, but I know it won't be." She caught her top lip between her teeth as her mind raced. "And what if—"

Luke touched his finger to her mouth to stop the words. "*What* and *if* are the two words guaranteed to make you crazy."

"If I'm not already," she said wryly.

"We'll work it out. Trust me."

"I could say the same thing to you." She saw the shadows in his eyes and knew she was responsible for them. But trust went both ways and it wasn't easy for her either. She once believed the sun rose and set on him, then he broke her heart and went away for ten years. That reminded her of something else that had been rattling around in her head. He'd told her he wasn't married and didn't have children besides Emma. But that was as personal as he got and she had another question.

"After you left, did you ever fall in love?"

Shelby couldn't believe she blurted that out. And he stared at her for so long she lost her nerve. "Never mind. That was intrusive and I didn't mean to be. Well, actually, I guess I did. Can't help being curious. You haven't said much about your life after leaving

Huntington Hills. I know about the army and joining the police department, but not much else. And
this could impact Emma."

"Oh?"

"Yeah. What if a strange woman comes barg-
ing in while Emma is with you? Is it possible there
could be a *Fatal Attraction* moment in her future?"
Shelby was making this up as she went along and
just bounced that last part off the wall. She wanted
to know if someone might show up who was important to him.

His mouth curved up slightly. "There have been
women but I'm almost positive none of them are
crazy. And I never dated anyone named Alex For-
rest."

"So, you've seen the movie." At least he had a
sense of humor about her inquiring mind. But he
sure didn't give much away. That was frustrating.

"What about you?"

Now he was turning this on her. "What about
me?" she said.

"Did you date? Fall in love?" The color of his eyes
darkened to almost coal black.

"No. Dating wasn't easy."

"How hard can it be? Someone asks you to dinner. You say yes." He shrugged those broad shoulders. "Nothing to it."

"So I go out to dinner, then what?" She raised
one eyebrow, hoping he would get it and they could
move on.

"I don't know. Maybe a movie next time."

"It's not that simple," she protested.

"Why not?"

"Because I have a child. If there's a third date I have to tell him about my nine-year-old daughter and that I still live with my mother. If I say that on the first date it never gets to number two."

"So you have dated?" The expression on his face was tense suddenly.

"I've tried. It doesn't go well, so I'm not really into dating." It was probably her imagination or wishful thinking but she would swear he looked relieved.

"I have another question for you. Not about dating," he said.

"Okay. Seems fair."

"Why do you still live with your mom?" He'd been looking down at his hands, but now met her gaze. "You have a good job. My guess is your reasons are not about money."

"I see you're taking your sleuthing skills out for a spin." She tried to joke but wasn't feeling it.

"Your mom seems to be healthy and fit. She doesn't need help physically." He wasn't letting this go. "So why are you still living in the house next door to mine?"

"I don't know. It was just easier to stay."

"Is that the only reason?" he prodded. "Is your mother pressuring you?"

Shelby hadn't really examined her motive for staying and he was right that she could afford a place of her own. And her mother didn't say anything about her preference so Shelby assumed she wanted her and Em there. Then Luke moved in and everything inside her shifted and turned upside down.

"Tell me, Shelby. Why did you stay?"

"Maybe part of me was waiting for you to come back." She looked away.

"If you wanted to know where I was, you could have found me easily enough."

"Probably, but then the other part of me would have had to face what I'd done. That I didn't tell you about Emma. I kept promising myself I would deal with it. Stand up to my mother and reveal the truth to you. But I didn't. Time slipped away and the longer it went, the harder it got." Tears welled in her eyes and one rolled down her cheek. Then another. "You got to tell Emma no for the first time. But there were so many good firsts that you missed, Luke. And that's my fault. It's unforgivable."

"I thought you weren't going to apologize anymore."

"I can't help it. I don't know how to make this better." Her vision was blurry as she stood and headed a little blindly to the sliding glass door. "Sorry to bother you. I have to go."

The chair scraped as Luke pushed away from the table. In a heartbeat he was there, behind her, his fingers curving around her upper arm to stop her from walking out. "No. Don't."

"I have to. I shouldn't have come over here—"

Emotion choked off her words and the tears just wouldn't stop. "I came over here to talk about Emma—"

"Really?" His tone was soft, seductive. "Are you sure about that?"

"Yes." She stared at a spot in the center of his chest, unwilling to test whether or not he could see right through her. That wasn't a lie but not the whole truth and she wouldn't be dishonest with him again. "And because the last time I was here you kissed me. I have to know. Why did you do that?"

"I wasn't thinking." He closed his eyes and shook his head, as if trying to block her out along with the memory of that intimate touch. Then he looked at her and the heat was back. "I didn't plan to. But you're so damn beautiful. You always were, but now... It just happened. I'm sorry—"

Shelby couldn't stop herself. It was her turn to leap without looking and she touched her mouth to his. She was tired of thinking everything to death. All she wanted was to *feel*, at least for a few moments. So she left her lips right where they were and savored the softness of his mouth, and the strength of his body next to hers. Then thoughts came tumbling back and reluctantly she pulled away.

She took a step back and forced herself to look at him. "I guess now we're even."

Luke cupped her cheek in his palm and brushed his thumb over the moistness lingering there. "I hate it when you cry. That hasn't changed. And I still can't help wanting to fix whatever is wrong."

"Even though you hate me?"

"I don't hate you." He sighed. "I'll admit I tried. But I couldn't manage to pull it off."

"Oh, Luke—" *Here we go again.* Her eyes filled with tears at his admission.

Before the waterworks could really get going, he pulled her against him and kissed her. Hard. There was no room for crying when instinct took over and she slid her arms around his neck, sinking into his kiss. She took his top lip between her own and sucked gently for a few moments, then did the same thing with his bottom lip. His breathing was suddenly labored as she tilted her head to the side and opened her mouth a little wider. He dipped his tongue inside and traced the interior. Everywhere he touched set off a spike of heat deep inside her. The feelings teased memories from a long time ago. It was a coming home kind of kiss that made her want what she'd had then.

Breathing hard, she pulled back just far enough to look at him. Heat and hunger blazed in his eyes and lit the fuse of wanting that had been sparking since she'd first seen him again. But that could be a dangerous step to take.

Shelby knew there was a better than even chance she would regret it, but she couldn't stop herself any more than she could hold back a tsunami. She slid her hands over his chest, down to his belt, then tugged at the T-shirt tucked into his jeans.

Luke put a hand over hers. "Wait—"

Oh, God. He didn't want her. A flush crept into her cheeks making them hot with humiliation. "I'm sorry. Apparently there's a general loss of thinking going on. I'll just go—"

He held on to her hand and brought her fingers to his lips as he met her gaze. "I want you, Shel. I don't know what it means. I can't make promises. It's just—"

"Complicated," she finished for him. "Yeah. I noticed." She tried to pull her hand away. "I shouldn't have done that and made things worse."

Luke pressed her palm to his chest, over his wildly pounding heart. "I'm not saying no. I just don't want you to have regrets. Between the two of us we have more than enough, so—"

He was being noble and that made him simply irresistible to her. She fell in love with him ten years ago but she wasn't in love now. That should preempt remorse, right?

"I won't have regrets."

He studied her carefully for several moments, then nodded. A sexy smile slowly curved his mouth. "Then let's take this upstairs."

"Is there furniture?" Her whisper was somewhere between a sigh and a moan. "Because, and I don't mean this as a criticism or deal breaker, there's not much here."

"I have the most important furniture," he said. "A bed."

"Okay."

He took her hand and led her up the stairs to the first bedroom on the left. Memories scrolled through her mind of being with him a long time ago. She'd given him her virginity and never regretted it, not even when he left, because she loved him. They'd cared about each other but he couldn't give her forever. And he couldn't give her that now but she didn't expect it. This would be enough.

The light was on in the hall when they walked through the double doors and entered the room. It had only a bed, rather a box spring and mattress without a frame, and the rest of the space was shrouded in shadows. Shelby couldn't care less. At this moment Luke was all she wanted or needed.

They were standing beside the bed. He was barefoot and she kicked off her low-heeled pumps. She smiled up at him as she slid her hands beneath his T-shirt and settled them on his chest. The dusting of hair tickled her palms and she realized there was more now than he'd had then. At her touch he sucked in a breath and quickly dragged the material over his head, tossing it somewhere. His dark gaze burned into hers as he slowly unbuttoned her blouse.

One by one he released the closures and his hands shook slightly as more and more of her bare skin was revealed. When the sides hung open, he pushed the silky material off her shoulders and let it fall to the floor.

Luke hooked a finger beneath her bra strap and moved it down, toying with the top of her breast. It was her turn to gasp with pleasure as anticipation pooled in her belly and tightened lower, between her legs.

He bent and kissed her, then moved to her neck before lightly licking a spot just behind her ear. Tingles danced over her arms and the sensation stole the breath from her lungs. Dimly she was aware that he'd unhooked her bra and brushed it away to fall between them.

Cupping her breasts in his hands, he rubbed the tips with his thumbs. A tiny moan caught in her throat as she felt dazed with pleasure, her world narrowed to nothing but his touch. An aching need strained inside her, demanding to be released.

"Luke—" There was desperation in her voice as she said his name.

"I know," he whispered before easily lifting her into his arms.

He settled her in the center of the mattress and quickly removed his jeans and boxers. Then he knelt beside her and unbuttoned her slacks before sliding them along with her panties over her hips and down her legs. Stretching out beside her, he traced a finger from the base of her throat down over her abdomen to the juncture of her thighs and the bundle of feminine nerve endings there.

When he touched it, the pleasure was so intense
that she nearly came off the bed. She reached for him
as heated licks of fiery sensation teased her everywhere. She remembered this, the way he knew just
how to touch her, just where she was most sensitive.
But that worked both ways.

She rolled to her side facing him and rested her
palm on his chest, then brushed her finger over the
contour of muscle. She kissed his neck then licked
the spot and gently blew on it, smiling when he
shuddered and groaned deep in his throat. Barely
touching his skin, she drew her index finger over his
abdomen and traced a circle until he moaned with
barely restrained desire.

"I can't take much more." His voice was harsh
with need.

"Then don't." She could hardly get the words out
but their gazes locked as understanding passed between them.

Luke got up off the bed. "Be right back."

A light went on nearby and she heard the sound of
a drawer opening. Then it was dark again and he was
beside her. He opened the square packet in his hand
and put on the condom. Then she was back in his
arms as he kissed her, taking what she offered and
silently demanding that she give him even more. And
she was eager to share with him everything she had.

She rolled onto her back and he covered her body
with his own, settling between her legs. Taking his
weight on his forearms he slowly entered her and

she lifted her hips to take him inside. Slowly she rocked against him, arching her back, asking for more, clinging to him.

Heat consumed her and too soon tremors started, pressure built, until she couldn't hold back her release. Pleasure tore through her and seemed never ending. She wrapped her arms around him and he held her close until her world came back together.

She smiled up at him and moved her hips again, noting the tension tightening his face as he pushed into her once more. One thrust, then another and he groaned before gripping her hips, holding her to him. He buried his face in her neck as his tremors slowly subsided.

Shelby didn't know how long they stayed like that without moving. Making love with Luke was the same, but new. She held very still, not wanting to break the spell. Unfortunately they couldn't stay like this forever and he got up.

The light in the bathroom came on again then went off a few moments later and he came back to bed. He pulled her against his side and she curled up in his arms. That was definitely new. A place to be together was a luxury they didn't have back then.

It was heaven and her eyes drifted closed. Her body was satisfied and her mind was tired. Before the thought of consequences even occurred to her, she fell asleep. She was snuggled in Luke's arms without a care in the world.

Chapter Thirteen

Luke woke up with a smile on his face because there was a woman in his bed. A curvy, sexy brunette with golden highlights in the hair that partially hid her face from him. The sun wasn't up yet but it wasn't pitch-black either. For just a few minutes he wanted only to look at Shelby and savor this unexpectedly different start to his day. Not being alone didn't suck. And it was peaceful—no undercurrents of emotion or tension. Nothing more than an agreeable calm and the satisfaction of fantastic sex. Just him and her like it used to be before he broke things off with her and ruined what they had. It had been the beginning of the end for them.

Now here they were because in a weak moment

he'd kissed her. In another weak moment he brought her upstairs to his bed. What did it say about him that he would sleep with the woman who'd betrayed him? She said it herself. What she did was unforgivable. And then she cried and that feeling of wanting to fix everything for her came roaring back. The line was blurring.

Thanks to Shelby, Emma didn't hesitate to come to him for dad stuff. Like the flashlight. And pleading for his approval of an unsanctioned mall trip. It was so completely normal for a kid to try and break through the parental united front. And that was his new normal because Shelby was doing everything she could to make things right.

And now she was in his bed. Where did they go from here?

He reached out and gently brushed her long hair aside to reveal her face. The flawless skin, full lips and impossibly long lashes that fanned her cheeks. She looked young and innocent although not as young as when they were together. She was all woman now. Her curves were curvier, her breasts fuller than before. Probably pregnancy and childbirth were responsible. He would have loved to watch her body changing as she grew bigger with his child. But that was then. Now he recognized that she was the mother of his little girl and damn good at it.

And he wanted her again, if possible even more than last night when she'd asked why he'd kissed her.

The truth was Luke hadn't been able to stop himself then any more than he could now. He leaned over and lightly touched his lips to hers. She moaned softly, an inherently sexy sound. Then she stirred and drowsily rolled toward him, pressing her body to his. Half-asleep she was telling him she wanted him, too.

He threaded his fingers through her hair and smiled when she opened her eyes. "Hi."

"You're here—" Her voice was raspy and she cleared her throat, then smiled dreamily.

"No, you're here. You dozed off."

"Why didn't you wake me?"

"I dozed off, too." He took her hand in his and linked their fingers. "How did you sleep?"

"Pretty good," she admitted. "As power naps go, it was in the top ten."

When she stretched, Luke thought he just might swallow his tongue. The movement was so unconsciously seductive he thought he might have a heart attack. Then her words sank in. "It was more than a nap. We've been asleep for hours."

"It's morning?" She sat up and looked around. "What time is it?"

"Don't worry. It's still early." He gently tugged her back down on top of him, her bare breasts nestling on his chest. "We have time—"

"You, sir, are going to hell for tempting me. I need to get dressed and do the walk of shame." She was forcing a teasing note into her voice as she pushed away and pulled the sheet along to cover herself.

He raised up on his elbow. The gray light of early

morning was enough for him to see her expression and he realized she wasn't rocking the same glow he was.

"What's wrong, Shel?"

"Nothing." The single word was too adamant, too forced, too everything.

"Tell me the truth." When her eyes narrowed on him he liked her expression even less and wished he'd phrased the words differently.

"Are you implying that I'm not being honest?"

"No. At least not the way you mean it. What aren't you telling me?" He winced at his choice of words when her frown deepened.

"I thought we put behind us the fact that I didn't tell you I was having your baby."

"That's not what I meant. You're deliberately misunderstanding. Picking a fight. Why?"

"This isn't a fight. I simply stated a fact. You don't trust me."

And you never will. That's not what she said but it was the subtext. He would address that at another time. *Let's try this a different way,* he thought. "Are you ashamed of sleeping with me?"

"Why do you say that?"

"Because you called it the walk of shame," he reminded her.

"That's just an expression."

"Yeah. I'm familiar." He sat up and the sheet pooled in his lap. He could think of a lot of things he would rather do in his bed than have this conversation but here they were. "It means you've spent the night at a lover's place and have to walk home and face people who know you and will disapprove."

"Come on, Luke—"

"No. Obviously we're talking about your mother."

"Okay. It's true that she doesn't approve of you."

"Tell me something I don't know. Subtlety isn't her strong suit. She's made her feelings about me very clear. But you're a grown woman." And he'd been thinking about that when he woke her with a kiss. This situation wasn't going at all as he'd hoped it would. "You don't need her permission anymore. To see me or to do anything else for that matter."

"It's a courtesy. House rules if you will." She tucked a loose strand of hair behind her ear.

They'd talked about this earlier but she didn't really address the question of why she still lived with her mother. When she said there was a part of her waiting for him to come back all the blood drained from his head and rushed to that part of his body south of his belt. He hadn't realized how much he wanted to hear that until she said the words. But now he needed an answer. It was important and he couldn't even put into words why that was.

On second thought it was obvious. It mattered to him that the woman who had wanted him out of her life still influenced Shelby's decisions.

"Why do you still live with your mother?"

"I thought we settled that before—" She glanced

at the small space of mattress between them. She was talking about the before-sex conversation.

"You didn't really answer the question then." He dragged his hand through his hair. "I think you stay because you feel guilty for disobeying an order to keep away from me. Then we had sex and made a baby. She gave you an ultimatum and you came very close to defying her on that, too."

"She was there for me. And for Emma."

"And you think you owe her."

"Yes." There was a world of emotion in the single word. She was breathing hard, but not from arousal. "I don't know what we'd have done without her. I was seventeen, Luke."

"I get it," he said. "But parents are supposed to support their children without conditions. We made a mistake and had a baby. She gave you a lot—a place to live, the chance to get an education and help with Emma. That's all great but it doesn't mean you have to pay her back with your life."

"That's not what I'm doing," she protested.

He blew out a breath and willed himself to calm down, to make sense here. "Tell me she hasn't been calling the shots your whole life."

"You're wrong about that."

"With all due respect, I disagree. You should be able to tell her you spent the night with me and not feel embarrassed or judged."

"She doesn't do that," Shelby defended.

Luke knew the difference between an outright

falsehood and denial. Her loyalty to family was admirable and Pam had made it possible for Shelby to go to school and raise a baby at the same time but that shouldn't come with a pledge of duty for life.

"When does it end, Shelby? When do you get to make your own decisions?"

"I already do that." Her eyes were troubled before she looked away. "And my decision is that it's way past time for me to go home."

"Even now she's pulling your strings."

"That's not true. I owe her the courtesy of not worrying her," she said quietly. "And I need to be there when Emma wakes up."

Luke knew she was right about that but still felt a little as if she was playing that card unfairly. Looking for any excuse to put him in her rearview mirror.

"Okay," he finally said.

She stared at him for several moments while holding tightly to the sheet that covered her nakedness. "Would you mind giving me some privacy?"

So the walk of shame was starting already. This woman who had given herself to him with such abandon a few short hours ago was gone. In her place was the beautiful mother of his little girl who felt she had to live her life by someone else's rules. And he couldn't reach her.

"Okay. You got it." He threw back the sheet and rolled out of bed, then walked into the bathroom without shutting the door.

Luke took care of business then got in the shower.

Part of him hoped she would say screw it and join him. She didn't. When he walked back into the bedroom, she was gone.

He had some responsibility for his part in failing her before, but this wasn't the first time she'd made a choice to exclude him because of her mother. He didn't feel any better about it now than he had then.

Staring at the bed where he woke up with her beside him he laughed. It was a bitter, angry sound because this day had started out better than any one he could remember. Sure didn't take long for it to go to hell.

Shelby hurried downstairs and out Luke's kitchen sliding glass door, back the way she'd come. She had to get out of there before she said something she would be sorry for while her emotions were all over the map. So back she went through that loose board in the fence. Was that only a few hours ago? It felt like a lifetime. They laughed, talked, made love and she'd been so relaxed and happy she'd fallen deeply asleep in his arms. Then she woke and felt a little panic about explaining where she'd been. One minute she was in his arms, the next things went horribly wrong. He accused her of— She didn't even know what. Being controlled by her mother? That wasn't true.

It also didn't mean she was going to make a lot of noise while sneaking, correction, returning to her house. She went through the fence and let herself back into the house through the kitchen sliding door. It wasn't locked which meant—nothing, actually. Only that her mother hadn't discovered it was open and locked her out.

She took off her shoes and went inside then turned to slowly and silently close the door. Suddenly the overhead kitchen lights came on. That startled and blinded her.

"Shelby Lynn, what's going on?"

It was never good when your mother used both of your names. And she did the same to Emma when her daughter was in hot water. A bad situation just got exponentially worse.

Heart hammering, she turned and blew out a breath. "Dear God, Mom, you scared the crap out of me."

Pam was standing just inside the doorway in her pajamas and robe. "I could say the same thing to you. Where have you been? It's the middle of the night."

"Closer to dawn." At least that's what the digital clock on the microwave said. She would much rather discuss the time than where she'd been and what she'd done. So this was what the walk of shame felt like. The expression on her mother's face was definitely disapproving. "What are you doing up, Mom?"

"Menopause."

"I don't understand. Are you having a hot flash?" The woman might be hot but something told her it wasn't going to pass in a flash.

"That's what you hear about. And the mood swings. But insomnia is also a symptom."

"That's right. I remember you saying something about that. I'm so sorry you can't sleep. Maybe there are some things you can do to help—"

"That's why I was awake. I was restless and came downstairs. Then I saw someone in the backyard and realized it was you."

"So, you didn't check my room," Shelby said.

"Like when you were a teenager? Maybe I need to start."

"I'm not a kid anymore." She'd just had a version of this conversation with Luke. It didn't go well with him. That didn't bode well with what was going to happen now. "I'm a grown woman."

"You're also a mother. What if Emma woke up and needed you?"

"I knew you would take care of her." Shelby winced when the words came out of her mouth. That was cavalier and thoughtless.

"Don't you think that's taking advantage of me? Especially when I had no idea where you'd gone, who you were with."

This confrontation brought back memories of being a little girl coming in late from playing with her friend. And a teenager who liked the boy next door that her mother believed was the spawn of Satan.

"My purse was here and my car is in the driveway.

Then there's my cell phone. You could have called me if you had a question or Emma needed anything."

Shelby stopped short of revealing where she'd gone. Luke's comment went through her mind. *You should be able to tell her you spent the night with me and not feel embarrassed or judged.* The truth was Shelby felt both.

Her mother folded her arms over her chest. "Would you have left the house if I hadn't been here?"

"Of course not." If she lived on her own, she'd have asked Luke to come over. "How can you even ask? You know me better than that."

"I thought I did. I used to." She pressed her lips together for a moment. "Since your car and keys were here, I'm guessing you were on foot. And you came back into the house from the backyard. Through the fence. Did you go next door?"

Resentment and a generous portion of guilt began to form a knot in her chest. This was feeling a lot like an interrogation. But she was also cornered and there was no denying the obvious.

"I went to see Luke."

"Why?"

"Because he's Emma's father," Shelby said.

"Is that all?"

"Does it really matter, Mom?"

"Yes. I'm worried about you." Pam took a step forward, then stopped. "It's just like before. When

Luke McCoy is next door you start doing things that are out of character."

"Is that a euphemism for things you don't approve of?"

"I've made no secret of my feelings for him. Remember what happened the last time you didn't listen."

"Vividly. I became a mother. It was incredibly hard and I couldn't have gotten through it without you, Mom. But I know what I'm doing. You have to trust me."

"It's him I don't trust."

Shelby played Luke's words over in her mind. *She's pulling your strings. You think you owe her.*

"What are you implying, Mom? That Luke is a bad influence? What am I? Thirteen?" She was caught in the middle and that put her on the defensive. "I don't have to ask your permission to see a friend."

"So he's just a friend?" Pam's voice had more than a bite of sarcasm.

"Of course he's more. We've already established that he's my daughter's father. But since he came back we've become friends, too."

"You've never been a good liar, Shelby. And thank goodness for that. I'm just trying to help."

"And I appreciate it. But everything is fine." If you didn't count the spat she'd had with Luke. She wished he had just let her go without any conversation.

"I'm not so sure. You had sex with him." Her mother wasn't asking.

Intimacy with a man was a very personal thing. Living under the same roof didn't entitle this woman to know everything Shelby did. Although she had to admit that because of the living arrangements it was pretty hard *not* to know what was going on.

Shelby hoped she'd gotten to be a little bit more skilled at hiding the truth. "Is it so hard to believe that we just talked about Em?"

"All night?"

"We fell asleep." That was true. "What does it matter anyway?"

Pam's eyes were especially uneasy and anxious. That particular look hadn't surfaced for years, not since Luke left. She was going into protective mode. "It matters because when he's around you seem to lose control. For an exceptionally bright young woman, sometimes you make decisions that aren't very smart."

"I know my own mind, Mom. I can take care of myself."

"So, you did sleep with him."

"Yes." She threw up her hands in exasperation. "What is the problem? He's a good man. He served his country in the army and now his career is in law enforcement, protecting the community. What do you have against him?"

"He made my baby cry. And I knew it was going to happen."

"That's why you wouldn't let me see him."

"Yes. He had a bad reputation and I was afraid for you." Her mother's mouth trembled.

"He went through a lot and was trying to figure out where he fit. But he's solid and dependable. I promise you."

"Good, solid, dependable men can break your heart, too, Shelby." Suddenly her mother looked ten years older as the sadness slid into her eyes. "I know all about that. Your father was all of those things until he left us for someone else and helped her raise her children. He made them happy at the expense of me, you and Emma. Now he's solid, and dependable for another family. I don't want you to hurt like I did."

"Luke is not Dad. And this is all your fault." With an effort Shelby took her tone down to the reasonable range. It had hurt when her father left and had no use for the ones he left behind. But not every man was like that. "Forget I said that. But think about this. Luke didn't have to take responsibility for Emma. He insisted even though he was angry that I didn't tell him about her. You forced me to keep it from him, Mom. If anyone has the right to outrage, resentment and indignation it's him."

"Shelby, I—"

"No, Mom. On top of that, you intercepted the letters he wrote to me when he was in boot camp."

"I thought it was best for you," her mother protested.

"But it was wrong, Mom." *She's been calling the*

shots your whole life. Luke's words again. "I didn't have a lot of options and you took advantage of that. If anyone is to blame here it's you. A lot of this mess is your fault. But I'm not innocent. The rest is on me because I didn't listen to my gut when I had the chance."

Her mother didn't say anything for a moment. But then her eyes went wide with comprehension. "You're in love with him, aren't you?"

Shelby shook her head. "No. I did the right thing and agreed to help him establish a relationship with his daughter. That's all. Nothing more."

"That's the only explanation for why you're defending him after he hurt you so much."

"I defended you when he wondered why I was still living under your roof." But she remembered blurting out that a part of her was waiting for him to come back. "He said you were controlling. And that I was paying you back with my whole life for giving me a place to live when I was a pregnant teenager. Is that true?"

"I admit it wasn't my finest hour, but I was upset when you told me you were going to have a baby. Do you really think I wouldn't have supported you?" Her mother looked shocked. "I would never have put you out on the street. I love you and Emma more than anything in this world. If I'm controlling it's because I'm trying to protect both of you."

Shelby was a mother and understood the overwhelming need to protect her child. There was nothing she could or would say to refute that statement. But suddenly the fight went out of her. "I think we should just leave it there, Mom. I'm going to try and sleep a little before I have to get ready for work and get Emma up for school."

"Shelby, listen—"

"I will." She gave her mom a tired smile, then moved closer and hugged her. "But let's do this when we've both had some sleep. I love you. Good night."

"It's morning."

Shelby ignored that and headed upstairs. She peeked into Emma's room and was grateful that her little girl was sound asleep. She went to her room, dropped her shoes at the foot of the bed, then rolled into it fully clothed. But sleep didn't come because her mind was racing.

You're in love with him. She couldn't get the words out of her mind. Things got tense earlier when he asked what was wrong and she told him nothing. Obviously her mother was right about her being a bad liar. Hence his comment: *Tell me the truth.* Followed closely by: *What aren't you telling me?* When she accused him of not trusting her, he didn't tell her she was wrong. Whether he would admit it or not, he couldn't stop resenting her for not telling him about Emma.

In this very room they'd made a truce to keep things all about their daughter. Falling for him broke the terms of that agreement just when he'd seemed to let go of his anger. When he made love to her, she'd believed he was back in her life the way he used to be. That feeling was magical. She couldn't stand it if he hated her again. That's what would happen if he found out she had feelings for him. So he couldn't find out.

Since she was apparently a bad liar, distancing herself was her only option. That was going to be a challenge.

Chapter Fourteen

Luke was looking forward to the weekend. He'd worked a few lately, part of paying his dues as a rookie detective. On the upside, he'd had other days off during the week and could help out with Emma when Shelby was dealing with work-related duties like meeting with kids, parents or developing a tutoring program for struggling students.

But now it was Saturday and Emma had slept at his place the night before. They'd watched *The Lion King* and Emma couldn't believe he'd never seen it. In a couple of hours she had a soccer game. A week ago he and Shelby had agreed on taking her together. It had been a few days since she'd spent the night for decidedly more grown-up reasons. He hadn't talked to her since. A text here and there was the only communication.

It could be that she was busy but he had a feeling something had shifted the other night. And not in a good way. Things between them had been tense when she left. Maybe at the game they could talk and he would apologize for sounding like an idiot who didn't trust her. He asked questions for a living but considering a suspect's feelings wasn't high on his list. He looked forward to clearing the air with Shelby.

"Dad, are you sure you know how to make pancakes?" Emma was sitting on one of the bar stools at the island, watching his every move. "You're just staring into space."

"Are you telling me to get my head back in the game?"

"Yes. I'm hungry." Her voice was just this side of a whine. "And the coach said we need to eat a good breakfast before the game. To keep our energy up."

"Okay, then." The dry mix was in a bowl and he poured milk in, then stirred it with a fork.

"Mommy mixes it with a wire thing."

"A whisk."

"Yeah. That. How come you don't?"

"I haven't got one. But I remember your Gran using one when she made pancakes for me."

"When can we go see her in Phoenix?"

"As soon as you have some time off from school

and I get the okay from my boss to string vacation days together. Soon, though," he assured her.

He and Shelby had talked about it and she promised to make Emma available whenever he could arrange his schedule for a trip. When Emma was out of school, Shelby would be too and he was going to invite her along. His mom had floated the idea and he liked it.

He loved his visits with Emma but somehow when her mom was with them, too, the unit felt complete. A family. Something he never knew he wanted until now.

"Daddy, I think you stirred enough."

He looked at the batter. "I think you're right. I'll heat up the griddle."

Because his daughter loved pancakes he broke his self-imposed rule of not buying stuff that had to be moved when he sold the house. Funny how a quick turnaround on it wasn't as appealing as it had once been. He got the electric appliance out of the cupboard and plugged it in then turned the temperature to medium.

"Do you think your mom has eaten yet?" he asked.

Emma's forehead wrinkled in thought. "Prob'ly not. On the weekend she doesn't like to rush. She takes forever to drink her coffee. Sometimes she forgets to eat until lunch."

"Should I invite her? This is our time together, I know. But breakfast is the most important meal of the day."

"That's what Mommy always says." Emma nodded. "You should ask her."

"Okay." Luke picked up his cell, found her number and hit the screen to dial.

She answered on the first ring. "Hi. Is Em okay?"

"Fine." Clearly she was keeping the phone close in case of emergency. "But we might have a pancake crisis."

"Oh?" There was no hint of humor in her voice.

"Yeah. Too much batter, not enough mouths to feed. Have you had breakfast yet?"

There was a brief hesitation before she said, "I did."

Luke couldn't see her face and wasn't sure how he knew this, but she was lying. "Maybe you've got room for just one?"

"Sorry. I have to bring refreshments for Emma's game. That means cutting oranges into slices and packing drinks in the cooler. But thanks."

"Okay. Another time. See you in a little while."

"Bye, Luke."

Vaguely uneasy, he hit the red stop button on his phone to hang up. One of the things about Shelby that attracted him the first time he met her all those years ago was her warmth. She was beautiful then and now, but her innocence and sweet nurturing nature made her even more so. He could tell without even seeing her expression that warmth wasn't all that was missing. There was no emotion at all in her voice, as if she'd deliberately turned it off.

He looked at Em. "Your mom ate already."

"Okay." She looked down for a moment then her expression brightened. "That means more for us."

"It does." He laughed because Emma wanted him to but he wasn't feeling it. "Okay, kid. How many do you want?"

"A hundred." The little girl giggled at her joke.

"You're hilarious." This time his grin was genuine. She made his world brighter and he realized something. Everyone said Emma looked like him but she had her mother's gift of humor, sweetness and warmth. He wondered why Shelby had turned those dials to "Off."

Two hours later Emma came downstairs in her black soccer shorts and pink jersey. She was carrying her shin guards and cleats to put on at the field.

"Do you need a long-sleeved T-shirt under your jersey? It's chilly out. And you might want to put on a pair of sweatpants then take them off just before the game starts." Look at him being all paternal. When did that happen? He'd been at this father thing for a few months now but it felt much longer and completely natural. All because of Shelby.

"Do I have to, Daddy?" She had a pleading look on her face to be let off the hook. "I left that stuff at home."

"Then isn't it lucky home is right next door." He remembered what Shelby said about part of her just waiting for him to come back. He knew what she meant because a part of him felt as if he'd been waiting for her to fill the hole in his life. "Run over and get what you need."

"Okay."

"And find out if your mom has the ice chest and snacks ready. I'll load them into the truck for her."

"Okay, Dad." She raced out the front door and across the two driveways, then disappeared into the house.

Luke walked outside, locked up his house, then waited by the truck. A few minutes later Emma came outside alone.

"Where's your mom?"

"She said to tell you she'll meet us at the game."

"Why?" Earlier in the week they'd agreed to go together but that was before he took her to bed.

"She said she's not quite ready and doesn't want me to be late. Coach wants us there early to stretch and warm up."

"Maybe your mom just needs a little help," he suggested.

"She said she doesn't." She watched him not say anything and her expression turned impatient. "Daddy, I'm going to be late."

He had an almost overwhelming urge to tell her it would be fine. He'd explain things to the coach because he needed to talk to her mother now. Then he got a grip. Whatever was going on would wait a little longer.

So he drove Em to the park and walked her over to the group of little girls all wearing pink. He shook the coach's hand, wished Emma and the team luck, then returned to the parking lot. Shelby wouldn't miss their daughter's game and Luke was going to intercept her when she arrived.

He leaned back against his truck feeling a lot like being on a stakeout. More girls arrived, some in pink, others in the opposing team's color. Finally he saw Shelby's compact car pull into the lot and he waited for her to park before walking over.

She exited the driver's door and saw him. There was a brief flash of something in her eyes, then her expression was blank. "You didn't have to wait for me."

"I'm here to help you carry everything."

"I've got it," she protested. "You should get a good place to watch the game."

"It's a park. There are no bad places," he said wryly.

"Still, you should set up your chair."

He frowned at her attempt to get rid of him. "You know I get too uptight to sit."

Luke waited for her usual teasing about his nerves of steel as a cop melted by pink jerseys and hair bows. But she didn't say anything. Missed opportunity or something else? He needed to know.

"What's going on, Shelby?"

"I don't know what you mean." But she didn't look at him. She turned away to open the trunk of her car.

"You're acting weird. Ever since we had sex—"

"Shh." She whirled to face him and glanced

around to see if anyone was around to hear. "You're imagining things."

"I'm a cop. We don't have imaginations. We gather the facts and fit things together to solve a puzzle." He was standing close enough to feel the heat from her body but refused to let that distract him. "Fact number one—you're avoiding me."

"I'm not."

"You're a lousy liar. That was all I meant the other night by the way. When you said nothing was wrong, I knew there was something bothering you and I wanted you to tell me. Maybe I could help. I was clumsy with words, but that is what I meant."

"Thanks for clarifying."

"Fact number two—you declined breakfast this morning." He held up his hand when she started to protest. "Don't tell me you ate. I didn't even have to see your face to know it was a brush-off."

"That was your time with Emma."

"And I was willing to share." That's what parents did. He tried to judge what she was feeling but her face was carefully neutral. Normally she was an open book and he hated that she wasn't now. "And we were supposed to go to her game together. A family. What's going on?"

Shelby looked away for a moment. "Her game is starting soon. We should—"

"Nope. Not going anywhere until you level with me about this."

"Okay." She nodded. "I saw a lawyer this week.

The one handling Em's birth certificate and putting your name on it. She asked if we had a parenting plan."

"A what now?"

"A plan for sharing custody. You know—" She thought for a moment. "An agreement about her spending every other week with you. Where she goes on holidays. Alternating them. Time to take her to your mom's which the attorney reminded me is out of state." She shrugged. "Legal stuff to be considered."

"It's been working fine so far." Annoyance trickled through him. "We don't need anything in writing. We already share. She comes over whenever she wants."

"But you're almost finished fixing up the house. It's nearly ready to go on the market and you won't be conveniently next door." Shelby tucked a strand of hair behind her ear. "For the record, you were right about me living with my mom. It's about time for me to—"

"Look," he interrupted. "I was out of line. It's not my place to judge. Your mom doesn't like me. She's entitled to think what she wants and I'll do my best to earn her good opinion. I didn't walk in her shoes and have no right to decide whether or not her way was right." He blew out a breath. "What I do know is that she raised you and you're pretty terrific. Emma, too. That was all under her roof so her contribution is there."

"Nice of you to say so." But Shelby didn't look at him. "Being neighbors has been good to ease us all into this new kind of normal but living arrangements will change. I'm just making sure your parental rights are protected."

"Because you think I don't trust you."

"Yes. And why should you? After what I did—"

"Let it go, Shelby. I have."

"Really? I don't know how you can." She turned away to lift a bag out of the trunk. "And I would never expect you to forgive me. That's perfectly understandable. I believe a parenting plan would put your mind at ease. It's the least I can do."

Luke could see she wasn't lying but there was something she was holding back. "Don't make this about me—"

"Even if it is?"

Before she turned away he was almost certain that a tear rolled down her cheek. He planned to find out what that was about but then she started to lift the heavy ice chest out of her trunk.

"I'll get that."

"Thanks. It's about time for the game to start." She took two bags filled with treats, napkins, cups and other things then headed for the field where the two teams squared off with a referee who was ready to blow the start whistle.

He would bet everything he owned that this was a deliberate attempt to detach herself from him. Why? And did the reason really matter? Luke had started to believe he and Shelby could be something again. Those two questions proved he had given it more consideration than he should have and that just pissed him off.

After school Shelby drove home and noticed the for sale sign in Luke's front yard. It had been almost two weeks since she'd seen him at Emma's soccer game and now she knew her comment about him being almost finished fixing up the house was spot-on. The sudden tightness in her chest proved that she wasn't as disconnected from that reality as she would have hoped.

His truck was gone which probably meant he was still working and she wondered whether or not he was having a good day. When he left ten years ago she'd forced herself not to think about him and it became a habit. Since moving back, he was on her mind day and night. If he knew she was having these romantic thoughts, any goodwill she'd earned with him would be cancelled out. Therefore, she was doing her best to stay in the neutral zone.

She parked beside her mother's car in the driveway, then got out and pulled her purse and big tote bag from the rear seat. She walked into the house and set her things on the floor at the foot of the stairs, then slid out the bottle of wine she'd bought on the way home. There was something she had to tell her mom and hoped the lovely chardonnay, Pam's favorite, would mellow the mood.

The atmosphere had been tense and awkward around here since that early morning when her mom discovered her coming home from Luke's. There was a very good chance the conversation she was about to have was going to make things worse.

"Mom, I'm home."

"In the kitchen, honey."

She sounded chipper, Shelby thought. That boded well for a positive start anyway. As she walked closer, the delicious aroma of oven-fried chicken surrounded her. Her heart squeezed for a moment because this was probably her favorite meal. It was the smell of détente in the air. If she didn't miss her guess, there would also be mashed potatoes and asparagus, too.

"Hi," she said, putting aside the guilt for what she was about to do. "You've been busy. Something smells good."

"It's your favorite." Pam smiled, then looked past her. "Where's Emma? With Luke?"

"No." Just hearing his name made her heart stutter. "He's working a shift I think."

"You don't know?" The woman's expression was faux innocence. Definitely détente.

"No. It's a need-to-know basis and I don't need to know. He's always available by cell if there's anything about Emma we need to discuss."

Now she was the one pretending innocence. Their communication consisted of completely unemotional texts. That should have been a relief to her because it guaranteed that she wouldn't give away her feelings. But not hearing his voice was its own kind of torture.

"Okay." Her mother strained the water from the potatoes she was preparing to mash. "So, where's Emma?"

"She went home with Karen after school and is staying for dinner." Shelby saw no reason to share that she'd arranged this so they could be alone. "She's getting dropped off later."

"Then I made too much."

"It will be good left over." She knew her mom was simply stating a fact, not deliberately trying to make her feel guilty. Still, that was her go-to response and confirmed Luke's observation that Shelby had pledged her life in the service of redemption for an unplanned teenage pregnancy. But, thanks to him, liberation was at hand. She held up the bottle of wine. "Would you like a glass? This is your favorite."

"Hmm. There seems to be a lot of that going around." Her mother smiled. "Yes. I'd love some."

"Me, too." Shelby got two wineglasses from the cupboard, poured chardonnay into each of them, then handed one to her mom. "There you go."

"Thank you, honey. What a treat. We don't do this very often."

Two could play the détente game. She touched her glass to her mother's. "To unexpected special occasions."

"Well said."

They each took a sip then a long silence stretched between them. Apparently it was going to take more than a little wine to ease the tension.

Pam cleared her throat. "So, how's Luke?"

"Fine I guess."

"You haven't seen him?"

"Not since Emma's soccer game. There was no game last weekend," she added.

"I thought the two of you were getting close." Again innocence and interest gleamed in her mother's eyes, a skill she used with a lot of success to extract information.

Absently, Shelby wondered if Luke used this interrogation technique on suspects he arrested.

"We share a child." She didn't want to discuss her feelings about him. "And speaking of that, I've consulted an attorney about putting his name on Emma's birth certificate and devising a parenting plan. We will share joint custody and all the terms will be agreed on and spelled out."

"That must make him happy."

Shelby had assumed it would, but he hadn't looked very pleased when she told him. Then he disappeared. The only information she had about him was from Emma who saw him almost every day. She told herself that he was maximizing his time, doing a big push to finish fixing up the house. The fact that the for sale sign was up meant that he'd been successful and would be gone soon. She wouldn't have to go out of her way to avoid seeing him. Oddly, that didn't make her happy either.

"It's the best thing to do," Shelby continued. "I

don't ever want there to be a question about his parental rights."

"Emma certainly is fond of him," her mother commented. There was no nuance in her words, no way to tell what she was thinking.

"That should tell you a lot about the kind of man he is. Kids aren't easily fooled. They see through all the baloney and call you out for it."

"True enough." Her mom sipped from her wine then set the glass on the counter beside her.

"The fact that Emma has taken to him so completely is a sign that he's not that mixed-up rebel anymore. He's a cop, one of the good guys. And a devoted father."

"For Emma's sake, I'm glad."

But she wasn't glad for Shelby and they'd already disagreed over this. Since Luke would never trust her, there was nothing more to say. And she couldn't believe how much just thinking that hurt her heart.

Not wanting her mother to see, Shelby turned away and pulled two plates from the cupboard and set them on the table. "There's something I want to talk to you about, Mom."

"Oh?"

She braced herself before facing her mother again and said, "I'm going to move out as soon as I find a place for Emma and me."

"What?"

"I'm going to look for a rental—condo, apartment or small house. We're going to get a place of our own."

Her mother blinked. She hadn't looked this shocked since hearing about the pregnancy. Clearly she didn't see this coming. "This is pretty sudden, isn't it? Why?"

Shelby decided to cut through the twenty questions and get straight to the point. "This has nothing to do with Luke."

"I didn't say that—" Pam's hand was shaking when she picked up her wineglass.

"But I know you're thinking it."

"If you want to spend the night with him…" Pam shrugged. "You're an adult."

"Mom, that's not what this is about." Shelby moved closer. "This is something I should have done a long time ago. And in the spirit of full disclosure, he did point it out to me, but he's not wrong."

"You saw that he listed the house for sale."

Shelby nodded. "But that was always going to happen. He's not leaving town. He'll still see Emma. My decision isn't about that."

"But this arrangement is working, honey. Emma is thriving. Is it really wise to make such a drastic change?"

"Change isn't necessarily a bad thing. There will be an adjustment, sure, but shaking things up can be good. Besides, it's not like we're moving to the other side of the world. I'll limit my search to rentals close by so she can stay in the same school. Give it time. The change will be good for all of us."

"How will it be good for me?"

"You need your own life, Mom. You're still young. Isn't it possible that Emma and I are a crutch, a reason for you not to put yourself out there? That you're afraid of being hurt again, the way Dad hurt you?"

Her mother didn't answer, but asked a question of her own. "Is this because I called you out on coming home in the middle of the night?"

"You said I was taking advantage," Shelby reminded her, "but—"

"I didn't mean it."

"Sure you did. And you were right. You've made it very easy for me to stay here. Very comfortable. But I realized—with an astute observation from Luke— that my constant resting state is guilt. I got pregnant at seventeen and turned your life upside down. I've been trying to make that up to you ever since."

"There's nothing to make up for," her mother protested. "I love having you here. And Emma is the light of my life."

"You'll still get to spend time with her." Shelby gentled her voice as much as possible. "And part of me knows that you don't mind us living with you. But another part of me is still that scared kid wondering what she's going to do. Feeling horrible for hurting and disappointing you. I have to go out on my own and be independent. I'm Emma's primary role model. How can she learn to stand on her own two feet when I'm not doing that?"

Unshed tears glistened in her mother's eyes. "But, Shelby, you're probably the strongest woman I know."

"If I am, it's because I learned how to be from a strong woman. And I will never be able to thank you enough for everything you've done for me. The best way I can think of to honor that is to show you I've watched and learned. I can do this." She smiled and forced enthusiasm into her voice as tears blurred her vision. "Just think, you'll have the house to yourself. You can do whatever you want. Think only about yourself. You should date."

"How am I going to meet anyone?"

"One of the volunteer math tutors is a friend of Brett's, the math department supervisor. His name is Gabriel Blackburne. In his regular career he turns around struggling businesses. His aunt owns Make Me a Match, a local dating service company. You could fill out a profile. Meet someone. Date."

Her mom gave her a speculative look. "Do as I say not as I do? Because you should date, too." The statement wasn't an angry reply. It was said with tenderness and love. "If your goal is really to move out and make a life for yourself, you should go all the way."

Shelby shook her head. "I don't want to."

"Because you're in love with Luke."

There it was again. But she didn't hear judgment in her mom's voice and was surprised. Still, admitting out loud to the universe that Pam was right wouldn't happen. Somehow that would give the strong emotions more weight and therefore power to make the pain of lost love hurt even more than it already did.

"Moving out will be enough change for Emma. I'm not going to start dating and really confuse her life."

"Hers? Or yours?"

"Of course I'm talking about her. Emma is my top priority."

Her mother nodded. "And you are mine. If you're okay then she will be, too."

"I'm fine, Mom," she lied. "Very excited about a new chapter in my life."

The chapter where she put Luke McCoy firmly behind her. That thought broke her heart as surely as it had shattered once before. When she was seventeen, pregnant with his baby, and told him goodbye before watching him walk away.

Chapter Fifteen

Damn it, he missed Shelby.

Luke had come home from work and changed into jeans and a T-shirt. Often this was when Emma would come skipping over. The equivalent of "Daddy's home." And, sometimes, Shelby would come, too, all in the spirit of giving their daughter a sense of family. Occasionally she brought him leftovers and he would ask her to stay while he ate. He loved that time with the three of them together and didn't realize just how much until it was gone.

It stopped right after the night they slept together. The next morning she was spooked about facing her mother who hated his guts. So he told her what he thought and she'd gone radio silent. Except for those damned unsatisfying text messages filled with perky, unsatisfying emojis that made his teeth hurt.

Now there were no late-night visits or sneaking through that loose board in the fence. No wine at the kitchen island while talking things over. No trips to the hardware store to look at paint chips. Come to think of it, Shelby's absence took a lot of color out of his world. If not for Emma…

Now it was parenting plans that spelled everything out and eliminated spontaneity.

Luke grabbed a beer from the refrigerator and glared at the opened bottle of wine that had mocked him ever since Shelby's last visit. It was way past time to pour that down the drain and he could make a metaphor out of that image. Instead he twisted the cap off his bottle and wandered over to the glass slider, then glanced at the house next door.

Lights were on in the kitchen but Shelby's bedroom was dark. Were the three of them eating dinner together? Laughing and talking about their day? He tried not to be envious but that was a bust.

For a while he'd felt part of a threesome—him and Emma and Shelby. Now he was on the outside looking in, just like when he'd loved her before.

After deciding not to torture himself, he turned away to wander and pace somewhere else. The house without much furniture screamed temporary and was its own kind of torture. Everywhere he looked were memories of Shelby. Her cheerful smile when she'd approved his paint job. Her sunny disposition when she refereed his first fight with Emma. The scent of her skin seemed to be everywhere and he wanted her more than he'd ever wanted anyone.

He drifted into the living room. There hadn't been a single change but it felt more empty than it had two weeks ago. Outside the streetlight illuminated the for sale sign in the yard. The real estate agent had called to let him know she had several very motivated and interested buyers and wanted to bring them by to take a look. Soon this limbo would be over. No more surprise visits or unexpected sex. Everything would be planned by the book.

He half turned away from the window when a flash of pink by the front door caught his eye. Emma's backpack. She left it here yesterday when she'd come to see him after school. Tomorrow was Sunday and she might have homework to do. After picking it up he glanced out the window and saw just one car in the driveway next door. It was Shelby's and that meant the dragon lady wasn't there.

Before he could talk himself out of it, Luke exited his front door and headed over to return his daughter's stuff. It didn't matter that she could get it in the morning. This was a thinly veiled excuse to see Shelby but he didn't care. Some would call him desperate. He preferred to think of himself as resourceful.

Luke knocked and a few moments later heard footsteps inside. The front porch light went on and then the door opened. His heart was beating just a little too fast as he anticipated seeing Shelby but her mother stood there.

He cleared his throat. "Is Emma here?"

"No. Shelby took her to a movie."

"Oh. I thought— Her car is in the driveway and—"

Pam glanced over then back at him. "She took mine because hers needed gas and there wasn't time before the show to stop for it."

Suddenly she looked small and sad, not at all like the formidable woman he'd always been a little afraid of. "Is something wrong?"

"That depends on your point of view. I was just thinking that putting off getting gas is a perk of living here with me that will go away soon."

That made zero sense. "What's going on?"

"You don't know?" Pam looked mildly surprised.

"No. Should I?"

"Since you're the one responsible for this, I would think so." Oddly she didn't sound angry, just really miserable.

"What are you accusing me of now?"

"Shelby told me what you said about her still living at home." She folded her arms over her chest. "I suppose being a detective has some characteristics of being a shrink. You do get into motivation."

He suspected she'd been watching too many police procedurals on TV but wasn't completely off base here. Except she hadn't answered the question. Her statements were random pieces of a bigger puzzle and he was getting a glimmer of the bottom line. "Is she moving out?"

Pam nodded. "And she has the audacity to take my granddaughter with her."

"She's Emma's mother—"

"Relax, Luke. That was a joke."

This was a side of Pam Richards that he'd never seen. Vulnerability. Still, he felt an overwhelming urge to explain why he'd said what he did. "I never suggested she move out. But she had to face you after we—" Crap. This wasn't awkward at all.

"I know you had sex with my daughter. At least twice." Again it was odd but she didn't look mad. She smiled and that was more shocking than if she'd slugged him.

He cleared his throat and was slightly horrified that his palms were sweaty. "I didn't plan that. She came over and we were talking about Emma. One thing led to another—" He met her gaze. "I'm not going to apologize."

"I didn't ask you to." She shivered then ran her hands up and down her arms. "It's cold out here. Do you want to come inside?"

"Yes. Thanks." If nothing else, he was damned curious about what was going on.

She stepped back and pulled the door open wider. Light filtered into the living room from the kitchen but she turned on the lamp beside the floral patterned sofa. "Can I get you something to drink?"

Who was this woman and what had she done with

Shelby's mom? That woman couldn't stand the sight of him, let alone invite him inside for a drink. Unless…

"No, thanks."

"I promise I won't spit in it or lace it with poison." Her expression was amused not hostile.

Again joking. He'd been so sure she had no sense of humor.

"I have a beer at home. But I noticed Emma left her backpack and I thought she might need it."

"And you were hoping to see Shelby, not me."

"Well, yes." Because he was tired of texting and tired of missing her so much it hurt.

Pam took the backpack he held out and set it on the floor at the bottom of the stairs. "Why don't you have a seat."

Now Luke was sure he'd stumbled into an alternative universe. But, why not? He sat on the sofa. "Thanks."

She sat in the small swivel rocking chair at a right angle to him. "The thing is, Shelby and I had a fight the night she was with you. She said this was all my fault and by that she meant what happened with you. And, no, you don't have to apologize. I do. And I should have a long time ago."

"Excuse me?"

"I'm responsible for you missing all those years with your daughter, Luke. I'm not making excuses but I want to explain where I was coming from." She looked down at her hands for a moment as if gathering her thoughts. "My husband left me for another woman. She was pregnant and he started another family with her. Whatever was wrong in our relationship, that was on me. But Shelby didn't deserve to lose her father and that's on him. He turned his back on her, too. So I was alone to raise her."

"I'm sorry."

"Not your fault." She let out a breath, then continued. "It was Shelby and me against the world, and then she told me she was pregnant and the baby was yours. I didn't approve of you."

"I know," he said wryly.

For just a moment the corners of her mouth turned up, then she grew serious again. "Forbidding her to see you, I thought I was doing the right thing for my baby. In the end it was wrong to keep you from yours." She looked down again for just a moment, gathering herself. "And your letters. I didn't look at them."

"If you read one, you read them all. They were variations on the same theme."

"Which was?"

"I loved her." He met the woman's gaze. "And I was an idiot to let her go."

"You weren't the only idiot." Pam sighed. "Keeping them from Shelby was wrong, too. I just wanted her to break off all contact. I was afraid you'd ruin her life. But I'm afraid I did that. It was so many kinds of wrong and I realize that now. And I'm paying a high price for those mistakes."

"I imagine you are."

"Thank you for listening. It's more of a chance than I gave you." She nodded. "I hope someday you can find it in your heart to forgive me."

He wasn't there yet, but this was more than he'd ever thought could happen. "I take it you never expected me to come back."

"That's true. But here you are." She hesitated a moment, then seemed to make a decision. "I did a lot of things wrong, but not all of it. I know my daughter. And when you moved in next door I saw the way she looked at you."

He sensed this was a turning point but wasn't sure whether or not it would kick him in the head or the heart. "How did she look at me?"

"Just like she did when she was seventeen and so obviously in love with you. I couldn't believe that she'd fallen for the bad boy next door."

"What?" He couldn't believe what he was hearing.

"It has to be said that you made some questionable life choices back then and she only had me to protect her."

The feelings of wanting to make her world perfect were as strong now as they had been then. "I would have given my life for her."

"I know. If I hadn't had a stick up my butt I would have seen it. That's what every mother wants for her child. And I'm the fool who stood in your way. And I'm sorry for that. More than I can say." Pam smiled with genuine warmth. "You're a good man, Luke.

Shelby always knew that. She defended you then as fiercely as she did the other night."

That meant more to him than he could put into words. "Thank you for telling me."

"It's the least I can do to try and make up for my mistakes." Suddenly earnest, she leaned toward him. "And I'll tell you something else, too. One can make a case for your poor decisions back then. The loss of your father at an impressionable age can't have been easy. Going into the army was a good move."

"It was my mom's idea."

"By the way, thank you for your service." Pam smiled. "But you're a grown man now. Not many people get a second chance. You're going to blow yours if you continue to be a stubborn ass. You can hate me, Luke, I deserve it. But don't shut Shelby out."

"I think you're talking to the wrong person. She's shut me out."

Pam thought about that for a moment and nodded. "I know my daughter. She's in love with you but the idea of it scares her. She won't risk not having you in her life and has pulled back. And I don't have much to lose by saying this. I think you love her, too. You could see that if you let yourself forgive her."

He did see it. The truth was, he'd forgiven Shelby almost from the first day he'd returned.

Shelby thought having a fun outing at the movies last night would bank her some goodwill with Emma when they looked for a new place to live today. It didn't. This child was very vocal in her disdain of everything. The apartment didn't have a yard where she could practice her soccer skills and she wasn't allowed to play ball inside. That was a point to her. The condo was dinky and dark. Her words and she wasn't wrong.

But the little house was cute, lots of light and had a nice yard. Emma simply said it was stupid. There was a lot of stupid going around but Shelby claimed most of it for herself. Last night went a little late and today her daughter was showing clear signs of not enough sleep. On top of that she was adamant in her aversion to this move.

Shelby was driving them home after looking at the last rental property. The next time she was doing it solo. If Emma needed therapy because she wasn't included in the decision, so be it.

"Mommy, why can't we just stay with Grammy?" The whine in her voice wasn't any more attractive now than when she was two.

"I already told you why." Shelby's patience was unraveling. She was tired too because Luke was on her mind all the time and made sleep hard to come by. It hurt so much that he lived right next door but was lost to her. As far as her heart was concerned he might as well be halfway around the world. "Look, sweetie, we've imposed on Grammy long enough. I should have moved out a long time ago."

"But don't you want to stay with your mother? You told me you wanted me to stay with you forever."

"That's just an expression of how much I love you."

"And Grammy loves us. She doesn't want us to move."

"Did she say that?" Shelby couldn't handle it if her mom ganged up on her, too.

"No, but I know it." The whine was replaced by defiance.

"And I know she believes it's best for me to stand on my own two feet."

Even as she made that statement, Shelby was well aware that Emma would use it against her. The next time she wanted to go to the mall without an adult. She made a mental note to apologize to her mom for all the times she was mouthy and stubborn.

Come to think of it, her mom had looked a little strange this morning. She'd said Luke returned Emma's backpack last night, then changed the subject. Probably the prospect of her and Emma moving out had thrown her off her game.

"Mommy, you know if we move away that Daddy won't be next door anymore."

"Yes." After braking for a red light, she glanced over at her daughter in the passenger seat. "And you realize that he's selling the house and will be living somewhere else no matter what we do, right?"

"He might not sell it. Just because there's a sign, that doesn't mean anything." This time her tone was part whine, part pout and 100 percent disapproving.

The light changed and Shelby accelerated without responding. What could she say to make this child feel better? The answer was nothing. Kids had to learn about disappointment and Emma had known his intentions from the beginning. Luke came back for the sole purpose of selling his mother's house. He painted the inside a neutral shade, including Emma's room over her obvious displeasure, so it would appeal to the vast majority of buyers. Everything he'd done had been with the mind-set of leaving. She'd slept with him knowing that and it wasn't fair or smart to expect anything more.

Shelby made the familiar turn into the housing development. After a couple more lefts and rights, she went slowly up the street, really looking at the houses. Most of her life she'd lived here. She went to school, fell in love, had her heart broken, gave birth to a daughter, graduated from college and became a teacher, then fell back in love with the same man. Moving away would be hard. Really hard. But also symbolic of her independence. She'd survived losing Luke once before and she could do it again.

The secret was out. Emma knew and loved her father which was the most important thing. Shelby would miss being able to catch glimpses of him getting out of his truck, bringing in groceries, working in the yard. But life went on.

And there he was out in the yard when she pulled her car into the driveway. How was it he could look so darn good in those worn jeans and an old T-shirt. She sat there for a few moments with the engine running while she memorized the lines of his body and the fit of that shirt hugging his broad shoulders. Her breathing grew a little shaky—

"Mom, look!" Emma was pointing to the real estate sign in his yard. "He did it."

"Did what?" Shelby saw the sold sign that was new and her heart squeezed painfully. He actually sold the house.

It wasn't a surprise that he followed through but Shelby's feelings overwhelmed her. She'd experienced this hollow, aching pain once before, ten years ago, but this time the awfulness was even worse. Before she could catch her breath, Emma removed her seat belt and got out of the car.

"I can't believe he did it." Then she slammed the door behind her.

Shelby watched her march around the front of the car and her expression was not unlike the way she'd looked that first day Luke came back. When she'd knocked on his door and demanded to know if he was her father.

Awareness sliced through her pain and galvanized Shelby into action. When she got out of the car, Luke was right in front of her with their daughter. Emma was glaring up at him.

"How could you?" she shouted. "I thought you liked it here."

"I do, kiddo—"

"That's a lie. You sold Gran's house to total strangers."

"It's not what you think. If you'll just listen to me for a second—"

"I don't believe you. You sold it to someone stupid. Another kid will be sleeping in my room. Probably a dumb boy." Her hands were balled into fists. "I'm glad you painted it that stupid, boring color because now they'll have to live in it, not me. But I bet they won't like it either. You make me so mad. I just—"

"Do not say the word *hate*," Shelby warned. "You're angry and hurt but you don't mean that."

"I kn-know." Anger drained away and tears filled Emma's eyes then rolled down her cheeks. "I love you, Daddy. I don't want you to go."

"I'm not, honey." He went down on one knee in the grass and met her gaze. "That's what I've been trying to tell you. I bought the house."

"You did?"

"Yes—"

"Oh, Daddy—" Emma slid her arms around his neck and hugged him so tight his answer was cut off.

Shelby couldn't believe she'd heard right. "I don't understand."

He looked up at her. "The plan was to sell it and buy something because I had to live somewhere. I already had loan approval and made an offer to my mom which she accepted. Her retirement is secure and I've got a house in a desirable area with awesome neighbors and the best schools. I hear it's a good place to raise kids."

"I just thought of somethin' awful." Emma left one arm on his shoulder and now glared up at Shelby. "Dad will be here but we're moving."

"About that—" Luke looked up at her, too.

"Daddy, I'm gonna go tell Grammy you're staying." Emma raced around the car before either of them could say anything.

Shelby stared after her. "I wonder how Mom will take that news."

"Maybe better than you think." He stood and there was something different in his eyes. Peace, maybe?

"How can you say that? What happened?"

"Last night I brought Emma's backpack over. An excuse to see you," he added.

Her heart fluttered, but she put the feeling aside for a moment. "And?"

"She invited me in."

Her eyes widened. "I don't know why I didn't feel *that* disturbance in the force."

"I know, right?" His smile was a brief flash before he turned serious again. "She admitted she was wrong about me. Apologized and said she hoped someday I could forgive her."

No wonder he was at peace. His harshest critic might now be a fangirl. "It's about time. But the house, Luke. I don't understand. What about the bad memories?"

"Yeah." He stared at his front door. "But there are good ones, too. Because of that house, I met you and we had Emma."

"That tore us apart."

"At first. But I've thought a lot about this. We were so young. If you'd told me about her, I would have done the right thing, even though I was leaving to join the army and get my head on straight." He met her gaze. "There's a better than even chance what we had would have been screwed up beyond repair by doing that. We'll never know."

She thought about how much she'd wanted to go to college and how hard that would have been under the circumstances he described. Resentment very well could have festered and torn them apart. She nodded. "A definite possibility."

"Again, because of the house we got a second chance. We're older and wiser and can put those painful lessons to good use." The intensity in his eyes was like a touch. "Unless I completely messed us up and you don't love me."

She laughed but there was no humor in it. "Love is not the problem. It's what made me bring up a legal parenting plan."

"I don't understand."

"I knew I was in love with you but we only agreed to work together to build your relationship with Emma. Nothing more. Nothing personal. I knew if I spent too much time with you, you'd figure out what I was feeling. You would be able to see that I didn't keep my word and hate me for it."

"That could never happen." He took her hand, as if the need to touch her was too much to resist.

"I'm not so sure. I was afraid of losing what little we had. And I wanted you in my life, no matter what."

"Done. I'm here. You're not getting rid of me," he promised.

"But what convinced you to buy the house?"

"Your mom."

Shelby blinked up at him. "No way."

"Way." He grinned. "She said I should stop being a stubborn ass and tell you that I'm in love with you."

She was almost afraid to ask but had to know. "Are you?"

"I am crazy in love with you, Shelby Lynn Richards. And I want you to marry me and move into my new house. Please." He looked a little nervous, a lot hopeful. "I want us to be a family. You, me and Emma. What do you say?"

"I love you, too." She moved close and turned her face up to his.

He pulled her into his arms and pressed his mouth to hers. She wasn't sure how much time went by before they came up for air but it was without a doubt the best kiss she'd ever had.

"So, this whole family thing," she said, "our daughter might have something to say. We should talk to her—"

"I say yes." The little eavesdropper jumped out from behind her car. "You should marry him, Mommy."

"I guess we have permission," Luke said, pulling Emma into the circle when she moved closer. "And we'll all live happily ever after in the house next door."

"On one condition," Emma said. "Can we change the color of the walls in my room?"

"I will repaint them in any shade you want."

"Okay," Emma said. "We'll marry you."

"Yes, we will," Shelby agreed. "The sooner the better. I've been waiting ten years for you to ask."

Shelby never dreamed she could be this happy. There'd been a lot of bumps along the way which made this moment even more satisfying. In ten years they'd never fallen out of love with each other. All it took to bring them together was a daughter on his doorstep.

* * * * *

Don't miss Teresa Southwick's next book,
part of the latest Montana Mavericks continuity
in October 2020!

And for more secret baby romances, check out
these great Harlequin Special Edition books:

For the Twins' Sake
by Melissa Senate

The Soldier's Secret Son
by Helen Lacey

What Makes a Father
by Teresa Southwick

Available now!

COMING NEXT MONTH FROM

♦ HARLEQUIN
SPECIAL EDITION

Available February 18, 2020

#2749 A PROMISE TO KEEP
Return to the Double C • by Allison Leigh

When Jed Dalloway started over, ranching a mountain plot for his recluse boss saved him. So when hometown girl April Reed offers a deal to develop the land, to protect his ailing mentor, Jed tells her no sale. But his heart doesn't get the message...

#2750 THE MAYOR'S SECRET FORTUNE
The Fortunes of Texas: Rambling Rose • by Judy Duarte

When Steven Fortune proposes to Ellie Hernandez, the mayor of Rambling Rose, no one is more surprised than Ellie herself. Until recently, Steven was practically her enemy! But his offer of a marriage of convenience arrives at her weakest moment. Can they pull off a united front?

#2751 THE BEST INTENTIONS
Welcome to Starlight • by Michelle Major

A string of bad choices led Kaitlin Carmody to a fresh start in a small town. But Finn Samuelson, her boss's stubborn son, is certain she is taking advantage of his father and ruining his family's bank. When attraction interferes, Finn must decide if Kaitlin is really a threat to his family or its salvation.

#2752 THE MARRIAGE RESCUE
The Stone Gap Inn • by Shirley Jump

When a lost pup reunites Grady Jackson with his high school crush, he doesn't expect to become engaged! Marriage wasn't in dog groomer Beth Cooper's immediate plans, either. But if showing off her brand-new fiancé makes her dying father happy, how can she say, "I don't"?

#2753 A BABY AFFAIR
The Parent Portal • by Tara Taylor Quinn

Amelia Grace has gone through hell, but she's finally ready to be a mom—all by herself. Still, she never expected her sperm donor to appear, let alone spark an attraction like Dr. Craig Harmon does. But can Amelia make room for another person in her already growing family?

#2754 THE RIGHT MOMENT
Wildfire Ridge • by Heatherly Bell

After Joanne Brant is left at the altar, Hudson Decker must convince his best friend that Mr. Right is standing right in front of her! He missed his chance back in the day, but Hudson is sure now is the right moment for their second chance. Except Joanne's done giving people the chance to break her heart.

YOU CAN FIND MORE INFORMATION ON UPCOMING HARLEQUIN TITLES, FREE EXCERPTS AND MORE AT HARLEQUIN.COM.

HSECNM0220

"Don't look at me like that, April."

She raised her gaze to his. "Like what?"

His fingers tightened in her hair and her mouth ran dry. She swallowed. Moistened her lips.

She wasn't sure if she moved first. Or if it was him.

But then his mouth was on hers and like everything else about him, she felt engulfed by an inferno. Or maybe the burning was coming from inside her.

There was no way to know.

No reason to care.

Her hands slid up the granite chest, behind his neck, where his skin felt even hotter beneath her fingertips, and slipped through his thick hair, which was not hot, but instead felt cool and unexpectedly silky.

His arm around her tightened, his hand pressing her closer while his kiss deepened. Consuming. Exhilarating.

Her head was whirling, sounds roaring.

It was only a kiss.

But she was melting.

She was flying.

And then she realized the sounds weren't just inside her head.

Someone was laying on a horn.

She jerked back, her gaze skittering over Jed's as they both turned to peer through the curtain of white light shining over them.

"Mind getting at least one of these vehicles out of the way?" The shout was male and obviously amused.

"Oh for cryin'—" She exhaled. "That's my uncle Matthew," she told Jed, pushing him away. "And I'm sorry to say, but we are probably never going to live this down."

Don't miss
A Promise to Keep *by Allison Leigh,*
available March 2020 wherever
Harlequin Special Edition books and ebooks are sold.

Harlequin.com